Lost on the Trail

Kenneth Taylor

Ridgeway Publishing
Medina, New York

LOST ON THE TRAIL

*To order additional
copies please visit
your local bookstore
or contact::*

**Ridgeway Publishing
3161 Fruit Avenue
Medina, NY 14103
ph: (888) 822-7894
fax: (585) 798-9016**

ISBN: 978-0-9792009-0-8

Printed and Bound by:
Ridgeway Publishing & Printing Co.
Medina, New York
888.822.7894

Table of Contents

The Hike

BILL'S SISTER CAME RUSHING home from school, full of excitement.

"Mother," she squealed, "on Saturday there's going to be a long hike and a whole bunch of us are going to take our lunches and hike the Long Trail through the woods. Mother, can I go, please? It's going to be lots and lots of fun. Please, Mother!"

"Well," said Mother, "I should think it would be all right, especially if Bill goes too."

"Oh, goody," Josie said, dancing up and down in her excitement.

Bill liked nothing better than hiking. He loved the woods and mountains, and the birds and the little animal friends that he saw out on the trail. So on Saturday morning there wasn't any boy in the whole town who was more excited than Bill. Mother had made the children a nice lunch, and Bill strapped his water canteen to his belt so that he and Josie would have something to drink, and there was a great big Hershey bar for each of them to eat along the way.

All who were going on the hike met at the school. There were ten or twelve there besides Bill and Josie. They were laughing and chattering as they waited for everyone to arrive. Some of them were gathered around Jimmy Gregory, who was telling a story about a little mouse that had gotten into his room at school the day before. Someone else was climbing a tree. It was a happy group of boys and girls.

"Hi, Bill and Josie! We're almost ready to go."

"Good," cried Bill and Josie as they came running up. "This is really going to be fun." Bill looked at the happy boys and girls and felt happy too. Today was really going to be fun.

But just as Bill was feeling most excited and the children were ready to start for the mountains, something happened that made Bill forget about all the fun he was going to have. In fact, he began to wonder whether he wanted to go at all. Around the corner, lunch in hand and ready for the hike, came Art Smith. "Well, come on," he said, "let's go. What are you waiting for? Follow me." And just as though Art had been asked to lead the hike, he started off up the street and all the others followed him, with Bill at the very end of the line, looking unhappy and sullen. It made him upset, the way Art was always acting so big.

But the day was too beautiful and the hike too much fun to remember his grudge very long, and soon Bill cheered up. Once he ran off the trail to chase a bushy-tailed squirrel that jumped from tree to tree ahead of him through the woods. By the time he got back to the trail the others were far ahead. Bill could barely hear them talking and laughing, as they ran and shouted in the crisp morning air.

During the lunch hour, Bill sat where he could look down over the tops of the trees to the valley beyond, and miles away to the great snow-capped Mount Baldy glistening in the sunshine.

Mount Baldy was one of Bill's favorite mountains. From the town where he lived, which was in a valley with hills and trees all around it, one couldn't see the snow-peaked mountains beyond. But from here on the trail, Mount Baldy loomed up massive and white even in the distance. Someday Bill was going to climb Mount Baldy with his dad, because his dad had promised to take him. Whenever Bill came out on the trail he always looked for Mount Baldy as some kind of special friend because it was always there, always waiting for him, always

6

shining in the distance.

After lunch, Art said they would go on up the trail for another half-hour or so, and then play games before starting back home. With Art at the head of the line, they left the open place in the woods and the high rock where Bill had been sitting, and started winding their way upward toward the peak. Most of the children had never been that far up the trail before, and it was fun to explore. Suddenly the trail bent sharply to the left. It was no longer climbing now but going along the pine-covered forest floor. Bill, who was lagging behind again, heard the other children's laughter and shouts somewhere ahead of him. But he wasn't anxious to catch up with them, so he decided to explore by going straight ahead instead of turning to the left where the trail did.

Bill always wondered why things happened the way they did. And when the trail suddenly turned sharply to the left, he began to wonder what was ahead that it was turning away from. But he didn't want to get too far behind in the big, lonely forest and he could hardly hear the children's voices any more, so he hurried to explore, pushing his way through thick underbrush. Suddenly he braced himself and stopped with a little cry of surprise and terror. Bill found himself staring almost straight down a thousand feet to sharp boulders far below. It was the canyon! The trees and the underbrush had been so thick at the edge of the cliff that it would have been very easy to fall off. He hastily jumped backward to safety. Then throwing himself on his stomach he edged forward to look down to the jutting rocks below and across the valley to where he could see standing there, bigger and more beautiful than ever, his old friend, Mount Baldy.

"Wow!" said Bill. "I hope nobody else tries to get off the path and come this direction, especially at night. I'd sure hate to get lost up here." He shivered at the thought.

Backing away from the edge of the cliff, he was soon in the woods and running as fast as he could through the underbrush toward the trail. He scampered like a rabbit along the trail, half scared and half delighted, until he caught up with the others.

Capture the Flag

BY THE TIME Bill caught up, the other children were choosing sides for a game called Capture the Flag. Art had read about it in his Boy Scout book and it sounded like lots of fun. Of course, Art was captain of one of the teams, and of course, he chose the biggest boys to be on his side; and Jerry, who Art said could be the other captain, took all that were left, including Bill.

Art took his white handkerchief from his pocket and went off in the woods to hide it on one side of the path while Jerry took his handkerchief and went off to hide it on the other side of the path while the children waited. After about five minutes, both boys were back. It was an exciting game and Bill could see right away that he was going to have fun. Anybody from the other team coming over to his side of the path to look for the flag just had to be tapped three times on the back and he became a prisoner and had to go to the prisoner base and stay there until somebody from his own side set him free.

So it was dangerous to go across the path looking for the flag. At any moment someone might step out from behind a tree and tap you! Trying to find the other team's flag and at the same time keeping from getting caught by the other team was going to be exciting.

"O.K., scatter!" said Art. And the children ran back into the woods on their own sides of the path to hide and wait for anybody who came across the path to try to capture their flag.

"You stay here and capture any of the enemies that come along," said Jerry. "I'll go across to find their flag." Jerry went dashing away through the woods, leaving Bill and the other children to hide.

"Yikes!" said Bill to himself. "He's going to get caught in a couple of minutes if he makes that much noise." And sure enough, before long there was a great shouting and banging through the brush and yelling. Art was saying, "I got him! I got him! Come on, Jerry, you've got to come with me now. You can't try to get away." And then there was silence again.

With Jerry captured, Bill realized his side couldn't possibly get the other team's flag unless he went across and tried to find it.

He moved stealthily toward the path, walking carefully on the fine needles like some Indian on the warpath. As he came closer he dropped to his hands and knees and crawled forward. Peering behind a bush he saw only one guard, looking the other way, with his back toward Bill. With one sudden jump Bill was across the path and had dived into the underbrush beyond. The guard turned around quickly but heard nothing more and decided that the noise must have been a rabbit or a squirrel. After waiting quietly for a few moments, Bill again moved stealthily forward into the enemy's territory. If he could only find that handkerchief!

It was supposed to be above the ground on a bush or a tree and visible from three sides. And the persons guarding the flag had to be at least 25 feet away from it in order to give the other side a chance to get it without being caught. A few minutes later, when Bill was edging his way forward, he saw a boy sitting on a stump; he stopped dead in his tracks and waited. But the boy on the stump didn't move. And when he turned around, Bill saw that it was Art.

"So," said Bill to himself, "the flag must be close by. Art must be guarding it. And he's probably as near as the rules allow. So he must be about 25 feet from it, one way or the other." Bill looked carefully in every direction. There was a high stump where Jerry might have hidden it. He even looked into the trees, although he knew that Art didn't like to climb trees. No, he wouldn't have put it up there.

Suddenly, Bill caught his breath and stared. Half rising from the ground he took a good look. Sure enough, peeking out from beneath the stump Art was sitting on was the flag. Bill almost shouted. That was unfair! Art was supposed to be 25 feet away from it.

Just then Art heard a noise and went to see what it was. That was Bill's chance, and he took it. Sliding forward as quietly as possible, he was halfway to the handkerchief when Art turned around and saw him. Letting out a roar, Art came tearing after him. But Bill got there first. Snatching the handkerchief, he ran with all the speed he could muster back toward the trail. Art came galloping and yelling behind him, closer and closer.

Just as it seemed that Bill couldn't possibly win the race, the path suddenly was there before him. With one last burst of speed he plunged across it and fell, panting, on the other side, safe at last.

But Art either didn't see the path, or, as Bill found out in a few minutes, didn't care. On he came and fell heavily on top of Bill, grabbing the flag away from, him, but giving Bill time to tap him three times on the back. "Now you're caught," said Bill, "come with me to the prisoner base."

"You fool!" said Art. "Of course I'm not going with you to the prisoner base. I've got the flag and it's mine. Now get out of here and shut up. If you say anything about this to anybody, you're going to be in trouble. You hear?"

Bill stared in amazement as Art ran back across the path into his own territory to hide the flag again. Suddenly seized with an idea, Bill jumped up and as Art ran heavily through the underbrush Bill ran quietly behind him and watched as he hid the flag again. This time Art put it behind a stump in a little hole between the roots where no one could see it at all. Then, knowing that the flag was safe, Art walked back toward the trail, evidently planning to cross the path to find the other flag.

Bill watched. Now was his chance. But he remembered what Art had said, and he didn't like the idea of getting into trouble with anyone, certainly not with Art. He stopped to think, and then, while he was trying to figure out what to do, he heard Jerry calling.

"Somebody come and tag me so that I can get out of here," Jerry was shouting. The voice came from a clump of trees not far away.

"First I'll try to rescue Jerry," Bill decided, "then I'll get the flag, because now I know where it is."

Bill knew there would be someone guarding the prison, so he decided to go around the other side and come in from behind where no one would expect him. He wriggled his way back through the brush and was soon able to look from a little hillock down onto the prisoner base where Jerry was sitting unhappily with a guard not far away, watching carefully for anyone who might try to rescue him.

"Hsst," whispered Bill just loud enough for Jerry to hear, he hoped, and not loud enough for the guard. Jerry looked around and a big smile lighted his face as he saw his rescuer.

Rushing toward the prisoner base, Bill leaped forward and grabbed Jerry by the hand just as the guard, hearing the commotion behind him, turned around and tried to head off the rescue.

But it was too late. As soon as Bill touched Jerry, the rule was that both of them could go across to their own side without being captured. Laughing and jumping with joy, Jerry rushed across the path with Bill right after him.

"Jerry," Bill said quietly, "I know where their flag is. See that big stump over there that's kind of rotten on top? It's just the other side down in a hole in the roots where you can't see it unless you get right there."

"It can't be!" said Jerry. "The rules say that it has to be in plain sight from three sides."

"I know it," said Bill, "but that's where it is anyway."

"That cheater Art," said Jerry. "He never plays fair. I'll go and get it."

11

Sliding back across the path and disappearing into the brush, Jerry walked hastily over to the old stump, and peering around the edge, found the flag and was just putting it into his pocket when the brush snapped nearby and, just in time, he ducked into a bush and waited as Art came back to see if the flag was safe. He walked quietly over to the place where he had left it and put his hand down into the hole. With a half-muffled exclamation he fell to his knees and began digging. But the flag was gone. Angry, he jumped up and ran wildly around, trying to find the one who had taken it.

Jerry sneaked out of the bush while Art was running about, and ran swiftly back across the path to his own side.

"We win!" he yelled. "Everybody come in. We win. I found the flag."

All the children came rushing back from where they were hiding on both sides of the trail. Those on Jerry's side were happy and laughing, and some of the children on Art's side looked disappointed because they had lost. Art didn't look disappointed when he came running up, he looked mad!

"Where did you find it?" all the children wanted to know.

"Over under that tall stump," said Jerry, pointing out to them. "It was down between some roots hidden in the ground."

All the children looked at Art, whose face began to turn red.

"That wasn't fair," some of the children exclaimed. "It was supposed to be where we could see it."

"It must have fallen out of my pocket while I was running by there getting ready to hide it," Art mumbled.

None of the other children said anything, but they all looked at him rather strangely.

"Well, come on," said Art, anxious to change the subject. "It's time for us to be getting on home. This game wasn't much fun anyway. Come on, let's go. Only first, I want you to see a cave back up here in the hills that has some treasure hidden in it somewhere. There used to be an old hermit up here in the woods who lived in the cave, and he had lots and lots of money and it's buried around there somewhere. My dad says so. He showed me the place and it's lots of fun."

The children were all excited at the possibility of finding a buried treasure, and they followed Art as he plunged through the brush. For ten or fifteen minutes, they stumbled onward until they began to get tired. Then they found a great overhanging rock with a cave beneath, big enough for someone to live in.

"You see?" said Art triumphantly. "It's here just as I said, and the treasure is buried around here somewhere too. My dad and I came up here and dug for it once, but we couldn't find it. Well, come on, you kids, we've got to get started back or it will be dark before we get home."

Little did Art realize how true his words would prove to be.

Tragedy Ahead

THE SUN WAS MAKING long shadows as the children turned back to find the trail again and their homes in the town below. It had been a happy day for most of them, full of fun and excitement. The woods were beautiful with gold, yellow and scarlet leaves. The sky overhead, when they could see it, was deepest blue with fleecy white clouds floating gently along on the light autumn wind. Here and there a squirrel or chipmunk crossed their path, and once a fat porcupine moved slowly along beside the trail, seemingly as fascinated with the sight of the children as they were delighted to see their strange, quilled friend.

The children were becoming tired now, and they were not running and shouting so much. Sometimes there was almost silence as they walked along, except for the breaking of the brush and branches as they plowed on through the underbrush and briers. It must have been half an hour before one of the children finally said, "My, but it's a long way back to the trail! It seems like we've gone twice as far as when we came to look at the cave."

"We're almost there," said Art.

So they went on.

"It is a long way," said another. "I wonder if we could be

lost?" "We're not lost," said Art. "I know my way. We'll hit the trail in a couple of minutes."

But they didn't.

On and on they went; some of the children were frightened now and thoroughly puzzled.

"That's funny," said Jerry. "I know we're going back the same way we came. It's bound to be straight in front of us somewhere."

"Of course," said Art, "it's bound to be." But he didn't sound too sure.

It was hard work beating their way through the brush without a path, and the brush scratched their legs and the brier patches hurt their hands. Some of the patches were so thick that they had to take long detours around them.

"I bet I know what happened," said Betty suddenly. "I think when we went around one of these brier patches we didn't keep going straight and we went off in another direction."

"Be quiet," said Art to his sister. "You don't know anything." "I do so!" said Betty.

"All right, if you're so smart, where are we?"

"Don't quarrel," the other children said.

And then one of the little girls began to cry. "Oh, I want to go home," she said. "I don't want to be lost. I wish my daddy were here."

Tears were running down several faces, and even some of the boys looked scared.

All this time Bill had been walking along a little behind the others. He knew they were just as lost as they could be, and he didn't know the way home either. An idea that scared Bill even to think about began to bother him. "I wonder where those cliffs are?" he said to himself. "I hope we're not going toward them. Half of us would fall over before we knew we were there."

It was a foolish fear, Bill knew. After all, the cliffs were in the other direction from where they were going. That is, they were supposed to be. But since they really didn't know where they were—well, Bill wished he had a helicopter that would take him straight up above the trees so he could see.

Thinking of a helicopter gave him an idea. He could climb a tree, couldn't he? If he could climb that tall one over there and get to the very top, he could surely see where they were. Without waiting to think any more about it, he ran ahead to where the other children were.

"Art," he called, "stop a while. I think I know how to find out if we are lost. See that big tree over there? I'm going to try to climb it and take a look."

"You're crazy!" said Art. "It's too high to climb and anyway when you got there you couldn't tell anything. And besides that, we're not lost anyway. We're going in the right direction. All we have to do is keep on going."

"I'd like to try," said Bill and ran over to the tree. Two of the other children boosted him up to the first branches and slowly but steadily he started up.

"Come on, you kids," said Art. "If he won't go with us he can just stay there and come home by himself. He's just taking up time. He can't help us any—and besides we're not lost."

But the other children didn't want to leave Bill up in the tree all by himself. "Oh, no," they said. "We must wait until Bill comes down. And besides, he might be able to see where we are."

"You' re crazy if you think so," Art grumbled, but there was nothing much he could do except wait.

Higher and higher Bill went, pulling himself up limb by limb. The children were soon left far below and he was up beyond the tops of the vine maples and the scrub pines. He was just a little scared. But trees were good friends of his. They always seemed to him to be holding their leafy arms to him or waving friendly greetings.

On and on he went until the children were out of sight in the brush below and he could barely hear them talking and calling up to him to find out how he was getting along. As Bill climbed the tree, he looked in the direction the children had been walking. Suddenly he caught his breath and gave a little cry; not a half a mile ahead of them were the cliffs. From his high perch, he could see how the trees suddenly stopped and gave way for a magnificent view across the valley to the foothills of Mount Baldy beyond.

But Bill had no eyes for the beauty. Instead, while he was right there hanging onto the tree he closed his eyes and said, "Dear Lord Jesus, thank You for giving me the idea of climbing up this tree before it was too late. Because if we'd kept on going just a few minutes longer, we might all have tumbled over the cliff. Thank You for helping us. In Jesus' name. Amen."

Even while he was praying, Bill heard Art yelling to him from far below. "Hurry up," he called, "or we'll go on without you!"

And the children cried, "Yes, hurry. It's getting late and we can't wait very much longer. Come down now, Bill."

"Wait," yelled Bill. "Don't go yet. Wait—cliffs are straight ahead." But the children didn't seem to understand.

"We'll go on slowly," they called. "You catch up with us."

Bill was scared. "Wait for me," he screamed. "Don't go on without me. Please wait. I have something important to tell you."

"Aw, come on," said Art. "He's just a baby, that's all. It will do him good to get a little scared. Come on, let's go."

The children didn't want to go off without Bill, but it was getting late and they thought that he could catch up all right. So they finally agreed. "Don't be afraid, Bill," they called, "you'll catch up with us all right."

"Don't go!" screamed Bill. "Don't go! That's not the right way. Wait for me!"

"Come on, you guys," Art said, "we've got to get going."

And so the children started out again, straight into the thick underbrush and the almost certain death ahead.

Art Loses Out

BILL WAS STUCK. It had been easy to climb up the tree, but now when he tried to climb down, he couldn't reach the next branch. Hastily he pulled himself up again and looked down wildly. There was the branch, but for some reason it seemed farther from the one he was standing on than it had been when he came up.

Perhaps some boys and even some girls who are reading this story will know what it's like to climb trees, how sometimes it's easy to stretch up and grasp a branch with your fingers and pull yourself up, but it's much harder when it comes to getting down. That's just what happened to Bill, sitting there in the top of the tree, while the children went on without him, straight toward the cliffs.

White and frightened, Bill clung to the tree. In the clearing on the forest floor far below, he could see a big raccoon moving slowly to its home. "I wonder if I'll ever get home?" Bill wondered, and then he began to cry.

Eagles soaring high in the clouds above the cliff caught his attention and for a moment he thought of a dream he once had —a dream of falling, falling, until an eagle had swooped under him and he had landed on the eagle's wings and been buried deep in the feathers of its back while it carried him safely down.

"I wish that eagle would come and help me now," sobbed Bill. Probably because he was thinking about the eagle, a verse from somewhere in the Bible, at least part of a verse came popping into his mind just then. "Carried on eagle's wings . . . carried on eagle's wings." The words kept running through his mind. God had said that He would take care of His children and carry them on eagle's wings. "Oh, if only God would send an eagle soon before the children have time to go too far. Or if only God would help me some other way."

"Lord Jesus," he cried, "please help me get down out of this tree safely and right away." That's all he said.

And almost as though God had just been waiting for Bill to ask Him, Bill had hardly finished his prayer when he heard a little voice somewhere below him. "I'm coming to try to help you, Bill," it said.

It was Josie.

Just how Josie could help him get down, he didn't know or care. He was so glad that he wasn't alone and that was all that mattered.

Up and up came Josie.

Glancing fearfully over toward the cliffs Bill began to think again about what was ahead of the children as they wandered along, straight to the precipice they didn't know was there. Bill had been so scared for himself that he had almost forgotten about everything else.

But now he began to feel frantic. If only he could get down, if only he could catch up with them and stop them before it was too late. If only they would stop and rest somewhere for a few minutes. If only, if only.

Once more Bill prayed. "Dear Lord Jesus," he said, "thank You that You are going to help me get down from the tree. But Lord Jesus, please make the children stop, or do something so they won't fall over the cliff." Then with frantic courage, Bill let himself down again toward the branch below. Josie was high enough now so she could see that his foot was just about an inch above the branch. "Just a little more," she pleaded with Bill. "You're almost there, Bill. Just a little tiny, tiny bit more." But it seemed no use. Bill strained himself with all of his weight and couldn't seem to get down quite far enough.

Then it happened. For just one moment, his toe brushed the very edge of the branch. Instantly, Bill let down his whole weight to the branch below, and, grasping the bark of the tree with one of his hands, he was safe on his new perch. "Oh, goody," cried Josie, not knowing quite what else to say. "Goody, goody, goody!"

Bill was too happy and relieved to say anything at all, but started climbing down as fast as he could. It seemed like a long, long way to the bottom, and it was. Branch after branch left his hand as he lowered himself to the one below. And all the time the children were moving steadily toward the cliffs. At last, he was down to the tops of the scrub pines, then to the tops of the brush, and finally he jumped from the lowest branch and fell in a heap with his face in the pine needles. He rested there just a moment, and prayed again. His prayer was very simple and quick. He said, "Thank You, Lord Jesus, but please—." And then he jumped up to find Josie waiting for him and Art's sister Betty too.

"Quick; quick!" Bill shouted to them. "The cliffs are over there where the children are going."

"Are you sure, Bill?" asked Josie. "I thought the cliffs were in back of us."

"We got turned around some way and we're going in the opposite direction from what we thought we were," said Bill as he started running.

The three children crashed onward through the underbrush, falling again and again as they stumbled across logs and tangles of brush at their feet.

Their faces were scratched and torn, and their hands were bleeding; they were crying as they plunged ahead.

"Oh, what if we should be too late?" said Betty. "And Art is the very first one at the head of the line. Oh, why didn't he wait for you, Bill? Why didn't he wait?"

"Stop!" the children shouted as they ran. "Art, please stop! Come back quick. We have something to tell you. The cliffs are ahead."

But the only reply they had was the echo of the forests and the crash of the brush at their feet.

And finally they could run no longer. Too tired to go on, too sick with fear not to go on, they fell exhausted, panting heavily.

But even as they lay there, far to the right and up ahead of them they heard a shout as the children were calling to them to catch up. With one voice they cried, "Wait!" Struggling to their feet, they started on again.

The children did wait. They were huddled in a cluster as Bill, Betty and Josie finally caught up with them.

"It's about time you got here," said Art crossly. "Come on, let's go. It's getting late."

"No, no, no," cried Bill and Josie. "We're going in the wrong direction. The cliffs are just ahead of us. Bill saw them from the tree."

"Bill's crazy. I told you that before," said Art. "There aren't any cliffs ahead. The path is ahead. Come on, you kids, let's go."

The children looked at Bill and then at Art. They didn't know what to do. Should they follow Art as they had been doing all day, or should they follow Bill? Probably because they were too tired to think about it, they slowly got to their feet and began to follow Art once more through the brush.

"Stop!" cried Bill wildly. "Stop!"

"Be quiet," said Art. "Come on, you kids, let's go."

Then something unexpected happened. Jerry was still mad. Even while they were walking along lost and scared, he had been thinking about the way Art had hidden the flag in the ground and broken the rules when they had been playing Capture the Flag that afternoon.

"Art shouldn't be leading us," he had been thinking. "He cheats. We shouldn't follow a cheater all the time."

"Wait a minute," Jerry said to Art. "Let's think about this. We've been going on the way you wanted us to go for an awful long time now, and we all know we're lost. Bill says he saw the cliffs ahead. I don't want to fall over any old cliffs. I think we've gotten mixed up some way and we'd better go back. Which

21

direction do you want us to go, Bill?" All the children seemed to agree with Jerry. They stopped and waited for Bill to tell them what to do.

Bill had never been asked his opinion like that before and it made him feel kind of funny and important. "We'll have to go straight behind us, back there," he said. "It will take us about an hour before we get to the trail."

"You're crazy!" said Art again. "The trail is in the direction we've been going."

Jerry finally decided. "I'm going back with Bill," he said. "All of you better come with us."

"Don't be silly," said Art angrily. "What does he know about it? He's never even been in these woods before. I was here once before with my dad. I know the way. Just follow me."

"No," said the children, "we're going to follow Bill and see if he can get us out of here."

Art was no longer the leader. That made him angry, but it made him even angrier that they were going to follow Bill.

"O.K.," he said, "go ahead. Get lost if you want to. The bears will probably eat all of you before morning, and I hope they do, too. But I'm not going with you. I'm going in the direction we've been going and I'm going to find the trail."

"Oh, Art," cried Bill, "please don't! The trail isn't there. The cliffs are there and you'll fall over the cliffs. Please, Art, come on back with us."

"Go ahead if you want to," Art said. "I'm going this way." And without another backward glance, Art stumbled on through the brush toward the cliffs.

The Long Trail

TO MOST OF THE CHILDREN, the journey home would live forever in their minds as one continuous nightmare. They were badly scratched. Their clothing was torn. Their feet hurt. They were hungry and badly frightened.

With Bill leading the way, they moved slowly back. In about an hour, as Bill had thought, they reached the trail.

They were very relieved and happy for a little while, laughing and shouting, until a look at Betty's stricken face reminded them that Art was somewhere far behind. The cliffs were there behind them, too. Oh, where was Art? Had he been careful as he went forward toward the cliffs—careful enough? Or had he plunged headlong through the blinding underbrush and seen too late the yawning valley at his feet?

And Bill was worried about something else too. It was getting late in the afternoon and was almost dark. Very soon it would be dark and they still had a couple of hours of hiking before they could reach their homes. They had no flashlights. How could they ever find their way back along the trail through the black night?

"We should hurry faster," he kept saying whenever the children began to show their weariness by slowing down. "Faster! Faster!"

And very soon night fell. It became harder and harder to see the trail ahead of them. The children held hands to form a long line, each following the one ahead, and so they stayed together on the trail. Bill, at the head of the line, walked carefully into the darkness, feeling the trail with his feet. When it became rough underfoot he knew that he was getting off the path and must turn back into the smooth place. That's how they kept going, even though the light was now entirely gone. But it was slow work. Sometimes despite all their care, they lost their way and Bill had to crawl on his hands and knees to find the smooth trail again.

Bill hoped his father and some of the other fathers would be coming to look for them very soon when the children hadn't returned home by dark. Perhaps they could just wait together in the path and someone would surely find them. But the night was getting cold and the mosquitoes were stinging badly there in the damp woods. Anyway, whenever they stopped, Bill kept imagining that he could hear bears, wolves, coyotes, and panthers circling around them, ready to eat them up. He didn't say anything to the others, but every once in a while he heard a crashing in the brush far behind them and it made him shiver a little. The thing, whatever it was, seemed to be following them.

On and on they staggered. When they could go no farther, they went on because they had to.

At last they heard a shout far down the trail and soon afterward a light pinpointing in the distance.

With new courage, they rushed onward now, still staggering, still stumbling, but with joy in their hearts as they knew that the rescuers had come. And then in a few moments more, Bill's father and some of the other men were there with sandwiches and chocolate bars, and flashlights to lead the way.

"Well, well!" said Dr. Baker, Bill's dad, "you children had quite a day of it! You must have gone farther up the trail than you realized. Or did you get lost?"

"Yes," said Bill, "we did." Then all the children tried to tell the story at the same time. When it was finally ended and the men had been able to piece the story together, they looked at each other gravely.

"So Art went on," they said, and shook their heads. "Well, we'd better get these youngsters home first and then go back and see what we can find."

The line formed again and the children followed the swinging flashlights down the trail. As they went along, Bill seemed to still hear the crashing sound behind them or sometimes to the side of them. When they stopped one place to rest for a few minutes, the noise seemed to be moving around in front of them. "Dad," Bill asked, "do you hear that noise? What is it?" His dad listened and said, "I don't know. It's strange, isn't it? I can't imagine what kind of animal would be scooting around here this time of the night. Well, I guess it's all right." But he looked just a little worried.

They had gone perhaps another mile when they came to a small fork in the trail. One branch went to Mrs. O'Leary's farm, which was down over the side of the hill. Suddenly a dog began barking furiously not far away and a woman was shouting something they couldn't quite hear. It sounded as though she was angry, angry about something.

"Now, what?" Bill's father asked. And he and one of the other men rushed down the side trail to see what the matter was. Mrs. O'Leary was still grumbling furiously as they came puffing up to her house. She was standing on the porch, angrily glaring into the darkness.

"What's the matter, Mrs. O'Leary?" asked Bill's dad, as they came up to the porch. "Is everything all right?"

"Everything is certainly not all right," she said. "That young scoundrel, whoever he was—Oh, it's you, Dr. Baker," she said, recognizing him. "I'm not sick today. I'm just mad as a wet hen, that's all. Somebody stole my lantern. I had it here on the porch, where I left it after I came in from the barn, and I heard Fido barking and went out to see what the hullabaloo was about and if some young scamp wasn't making off with my lantern. Fido was tied up so all he could do was roar around and I guess I'm just as glad, because there's no telling what he would have done to the child if he had gotten hold of him. But I do hate to lose my lantern."

"Oh," said Dr. Baker, "if everything is all right I guess we'll be on our way. We heard you shouting and thought we'd come in and see."

"And I sure do appreciate it, doctor. Thank you very much. But I'm all right. Nobody ever bothers much with an old lady like me and I get along first rate for the most part."

So Bill's dad and the other man went back to the others waiting on the trail. "Everything's all right," they said. "She says somebody stole her lantern from the porch. Lucky for him the dog was tied up, or I might have had quite a case on my hands trying to put him together again. And," he said suddenly, "whoever the scamp is, I think he is ahead of us on the trail. See that light down there?" and he pointed into the darkness of the trail ahead where a little pin point of light bobbed up and down and someone seemed to be running along the trail toward the village. He was too far ahead to catch up with and he soon disappeared where the trail bent down over a hill.

Only a little way now and they would be off the trail and back in their own warm homes. The children felt better with every step.

Then at last the moment arrived they had awaited so long. Out of the woods they came and through a little meadow until a street light was shining in front of them. They were at the bottom of the trail where it met the River Road. A great cheer went up and they raced to see who could get to the road first. Laughing and shouting, they waited for each other beneath the street light.

And then something happened that they could hardly believe, even though they could see it. Betty saw him first. She gave a squeal of joy and rushed over to the boy sitting nonchalantly under the street lamp. His clothes were badly torn and his hands and face badly scratched. And it was still a sullen face.

"Well!" said Art, for it was Art, "so you finally made it, did you? I told you, you were going the wrong way. If you had followed me you would have been here two hours ago. I've just

26

been sitting here waiting for you."

"You went the opposite direction and got here two hours ahead of us?" asked Bill.

"Sure," said Art. "You've just got to know your way around, that's all.

All the children looked surprised. They couldn't see how Art could go the other way and be down the trail first.

"Say," said Jerry suddenly, "whose lantern is that over there in the ditch by the side of the road?"

Art looked startled. "How should I know?" he asked. "It's just an old lantern lying there, I guess. Why ask me?"

"Because," said Jerry slowly, "some boy stole Mrs. O'Leary's lantern back there a little while ago, right after something had crashed through the underbrush and gone around us— something that had been following us all the way. Now I see what happened! After we turned around, you sneaked along behind us. You stole Mrs. O'Leary's lantern and that's how you got here ahead of us. No wonder we kept hearing that crashing noise along the trail all the way. You cheater, you! It's sure lucky Bill knew the way."

Art's eyes blazed with fury as he glared at Bill. "You're responsible for all this," he said. "And you'll get paid back too. You just wait and see." And with a final angry look, Art dashed off down the street to his home.

The Hero

I T WAS AN EXCITED GROUP of children that met in little groups on the school ground Monday morning before school began. The boys and girls who had been on the hike each tried to tell more than anyone else about their experiences on Saturday. And soon the school ground was filled with the story of Bill's heroism.

When Art swaggered down to the school grounds as usual with his ball and bat, the boys didn't run over to him as they usually did. Instead they stood around and stared. "He's a thief," somebody said. "He stole Mrs. O'Leary's lantern."

"Yeah," said somebody else, "and he lied about getting back to town first by going some other way, when all he did was to follow the other kids back."

"I don't want to play with him," said somebody else.

So Art found himself alone, and it shocked him terribly. It had never crossed his mind, for some reason, that the other children would care about his actions on Saturday. He thought they would have forgotten all about it. He thought he could come back and still be the bully and the boss of the school grounds; and that he would have his revenge on Bill by making fun of him. But it didn't work that way.

Even the teacher seemed against him. She asked one of the

children to tell about the big adventure.

"Aw, why did she have to do that?" said Art to himself. "Why couldn't she just forget about it?"

The child who told the story didn't talk about Art, much to his relief, but he noticed all the children looking at him and his face got red.

It was an entirely new experience for Art not to be the leader, and a very painful one. He didn't like it at all.

At recess time he tried again. He said, "Come on, you guys, let's play ball." But nothing happened. The boys just stood around looking at him. One of them said, "Naw, we don't want to play today."

And under his breath another one said, "At least not with you."

So Art took his ball and bat back to the cloakroom and wandered off by himself to the edge of the school grounds. His anger became a jealous fury as he saw the friendly looks that were directed toward Bill.

"He's not going to get away with that," said Art grimly to himself. "If it's the last thing I do, I'm going to get even with Bill." And sitting down under a tree he sat staring while his thoughts raced along—dark thoughts of how he could get even with the boy who had done him no harm.

It is written in the Bible that Satan entered into Judas Iscariot, the disciple who led the soldiers to Jesus to capture Him. And it almost seemed that at that moment, as Art sat there thinking, Satan was entering into his heart and mind in a new way. Art didn't have the Lord Jesus in his heart to keep Satan away and to help him think kind thoughts instead of evil ones.

And when someone lets Satan come into his heart, instead of inviting Jesus in, there is sure to be trouble. And the trouble will not be only for someone else, but there is sure to be even more terrible trouble for that boy who is thinking the wrong thoughts.

Family Hour at Bill's House

B ILL ARRIVED HOME from school that night much later than usual, but tired and happy. To have suddenly become the leader and hero was such an amazing experience that he didn't quite know what to do about it.

"Hi, Bill," the boys and girls had called to him as they were walking home, even when they were across the street. "Come on over and walk with us." Usually they wouldn't have noticed him at all.

And the teachers, who always liked Bill anyway because he was a good student, seemed especially happy about him today after hearing the glowing reports of the Saturday's trip. "Well, Bill," said Miss Edelman, "I want to congratulate you and your clear thinking last Saturday on that hike. It was a good job well done."

And Mr. Bruce, who was both a coach and a teacher, stopped him in the hall and said, "Well, young fellow, I've been hearing some good things about you today. A man of your ability ought to be good on our baseball team. You get out there and practice. Practice makes perfect, you know."

"I like baseball," Bill said, "but I'm just no good at playing it."

"Well, then," said Mr. Bruce, "don't worry about it. But you still can go out and have some fun even though you'll never make a baseball player. And after all it's a lot more important to be able to rescue children from falling over cliffs than it is to be the best baseball player in the world!" Then he winked at Bill and gave him a pat on the shoulder.

But best of all was when he got home and Dad said, "Say, son, did you know that you're a hero? Every dad and mother I've seen today has been telling me what a wonderful son I have. I'm beginning to feel that I must be a pretty good fellow to produce such a fine son!"

"Aw, cut it out, Dad," said Bill as he blushed with pleasure.

"Oh, go ahead and say some more things like that," said Josie teasingly. "He really likes it a lot."

"Now, Josie," said Mother, "don't be teasing Bill. He did a very fine thing and we're all proud of him."

"Sure, I'm proud of him too," said Josie, "but I'm not going to tell him about it. After all everybody else has already told him about it all day long, at school."

"You know what I think?" said Bill. "I think people ought not to say things like that anyway, because after all the Lord gave me the idea of climbing the tree and He helped me get down again and everything. So why should they keep acting like I did something great?"

"I guess you're right," said Dad. "We certainly do want to keep on thanking our heavenly Father for the way He took care of you children."

After supper the family gathered together as usual in front of the big fireplace in the living room, where they had their Bible reading and prayer. Josie passed around the hymnbooks and Bill got the Bible for Dad to read. Josie sat on a cushion next to the fire, and Bill, Daddy and Mother sat on the davenport.

"Let's sing a song of praise to the Lord," suggested Dr. Baker. "We thanked Him yesterday but I don't think it would hurt to thank Him again, do you?"

"I have an idea," said Josie. "Let's sing the doxology." The doxology wasn't in the book, but everyone knew it so they all sang together:

31

"Praise God, from whom all blessings flow;
Praise Him, all creatures here below;
Praise Him above, ye heavenly host;
Praise Father, Son, and Holy Ghost! Amen."

"I know another praise song," said Bill. "It's one we learned in Sunday school. I'll try to sing it for you." So Bill stood up and sang. His singing wasn't too good (Josie said that he didn't sing quite straight), but at least he got the idea of the tune, and this is the way the words went:

"Praise the Saviour, ye who know Him,
Who can tell how much we owe Him?
Gladly let us render to Him
All we are and have."

Then they sang the old hymn, "Safely through another week, God has brought us on our way."

After the singing, Dr. Baker read from the Bible. For several weeks, they had been reading each night from the parts of the Bible that told about Jesus and the things He did, and then they talked about it. Tonight they read from the Book of Matthew. As Father was reading, Bill seemed to listen especially carefully when he heard the words, "Pray for them that despitefully use you." After the reading, Bill said, "Dad, I think we ought to pray for Art. The children treated him real mean today, and he's not used to it. If only Art would become a Christian, everything would be all right. I sure wish he knew about Jesus!"

"Well, I suspect maybe no one has ever told him about Jesus," said Dr. Baker. "And if they have, sometimes it takes more than one telling before a person comes to understand. I agree with you, we should pray for him."

"Dad," Josie said, "I don't like the way Art keeps talking about Bill. He said he's going to pay him back. Do you think he'll try to hurt Bill some way?"

"I doubt it," Bill's dad said with a little laugh, "I'm afraid Art is something of a bully, and usually bullies are more noise than anything else. They talk a lot, but don't do very much about it. What's really the matter with them is they're rather scared themselves, but they don't like other people to know about it, so they just act tough and pretend they're very important. That's what makes them bullies, and if Art does try some funny business, Bill can probably run faster than Art anyway!"

Bill had been worried about it too, and he was glad that Josie had asked Dad. Since Dad wasn't worried, he guessed he didn't need to be either. Each member of the family made a special point to pray for Art that evening, that he might come to know the Lord Jesus as his Saviour. "And bless Betty too," added Josie, "because I don't think she knows about Jesus either."

After that, Dr. Baker prayed and asked God to help the President and the missionaries, the church, Art and his family, and the pastor, as he always did. When he had said the last "Amen," it was almost time for Bill and Josie to run on upstairs to bed.

"Could we please have a swing in the elm tree first?" asked Josie. "Oh, boy!" said Bill. "Would you push us, Dad?"

If there was anything Bill and Josie liked, it was to swing in the elm tree down by the road. And if there's anything they liked better than that, it was to have their dad push them because he could get them up so high that they could kick the branches.

"O.K.," said Dad, "come along with us, Mother, and watch the fun."

It was Josie's turn first, and Dad pushed her as high as he could in the regular way. "Now, look out," he said. "I'm going to start pushing you by your feet." Josie squealed with delight as her father pulled down on her ankles and sent Josie sailing high into the sky. Again and again he pulled as she went higher and higher.

"I touched them!" said Josie at last. "I touched the branch. Now let the old cat die." So Daddy quit pushing and Josie went slower and slower until she could jump out. Then it was Bill's turn.

But after the fun was over, and they were walking back to the house, something rather strange happened that bothered Bill.

Bill looked back and saw a boy standing on the sidewalk across the street staring at the swing. Bill was surprised. Why would anyone be standing there just looking at a swing? Who was it, anyway? The boy was too far away to see very well because it was getting dark, but it looked like Art.

Bill went into the house, but when he got up to his room he looked out the window and the boy was still standing there, looking at the tree. Then he turned around and walked away. He was whistling as he went up the street.

The Plot

ART GOT HOME from school earlier than usual that Monday afternoon. He hadn't stayed around school to play as he usually did. He knew better than to try. He knew the other boys wouldn't like it. Maybe they wouldn't have said anything, but they wouldn't have welcomed him either. As soon as he got home, he went up to his room and thought about his troubles. One thing he knew for sure: it had been Bill's fault. If Bill hadn't gone on the hike, everything would have been all right.

"But would it?" a voice somewhere inside him asked. "Would it have been all right to fall over the cliffs? Would it have been all right if you had been responsible for all the other children being killed or badly hurt?"

"They wouldn't have been hurt," argued Art hotly. "I was going the right way all the time. Bill is just a know-it-all, that's all."

"And if you were going the right way, then why did you turn around and sneak along in back of the other children?" the voice asked. Art knew the answer but instead of being sorry, he became even more angry.

"I'll get even with him," Art said to himself. "Bill's going to be mighty sorry he ever went on that hike."

"Get even with him for what?" asked the voice, deep down

inside Art somewhere.

"Oh, I don't know," Art said, and threw himself down on his bed and shed hot tears. He was tired of it all, sick of himself, both sorry and angry at the same time.

And when his mother called him down to supper, it didn't help any at all when Betty said, "Mother, all the boys were laughing at Art today because he got lost on the hike last Saturday and then tried to pretend that he got home first."

"Laughing at him, were they?" said Art's father. "Well, I'll just tell you what to do about that. You just go and poke them all in the nose. That'll teach them to laugh at you."

As usual, it was an unhappy sort of meal. Art ate as fast as he could and got out of the house. There would be no baseball for him tonight and he wondered whether there would be tomorrow night, or as a matter of fact, whether he would ever want to play baseball with the boys again at all—rather, whether they would want to play with him. He wandered aimlessly up the street wondering what to do until bedtime. Crossing the bridge, he stopped for a while to watch the water rushing by below. Once he had taken some kittens and put them in a sack and thrown them over the bridge at that very spot.

Thinking about it gave him an idea. "I wonder if Bill has any pet kittens or anything I could catch and drown?" he thought. "That would sure pay him back good."

And just then, he thought of something else. Only a few days ago a man had jumped into the water from the bridge, just about where he was standing, and had been drowned. The police said the man had been unhappy and wanted to die. Art didn't like to think about it at all. He didn't ever want to die. For one thing, he didn't know where he would go when he died, and it was all so vague and scary and dark and terrible. The time he had gone to Sunday school the teacher had talked about there being two roads, one of them going to Heaven and the other going to a terrible place called Hell. But somehow he had forgotten just where the two roads were and how to get to Heaven. It was something about Jesus, he thought, but it was all so long ago and the teacher somehow hadn't made it very clear.

Standing there on the bridge and looking at the water below terrified him now, and he wished he could remember what the teacher had said. Maybe he should go again sometime and ask her, if she was still there. "But no," he thought angrily, "that's the class Bill is in; I would never go there."

Thinking of Bill made him think again of the kittens. Bill's house was only a couple of blocks away and so Art decided to wander over and look around. Even if he couldn't see any kittens, maybe when he was there he could think of some other way to get his revenge.

As he moved along the quiet streets, he heard shouting and laughter in Bill's yard, so he slowed down and went across the street where he could see what was happening without anyone seeing him. There was Bill shouting with laughter as his father pushed him higher and higher in the swing until Bill finally touched the branches.

"I wish my dad would push me on a swing sometime," thought Art to himself. "Bill had better watch out going so high," he thought, "or that rope is going to break and he's going to get hurt."

Just as he thought that, suddenly down inside him it seemed he heard a voice talking to him, a rough sort of voice that Art didn't like very well. It wasn't at all the same voice that had been talking to him earlier that day when he was up in his room after school. No, this was a wicked voice that said, "Well, so you finally thought of it, did you?"

"Thought of what?" asked Art.

"Thought of a way to get back at Bill," said the voice. "So it would be dangerous if the rope broke, would it? Well, I suppose you could do something about that. Ropes can be cut, can't they? And also they can be partly cut so that they won't break until somebody is swinging on them."

"But I wouldn't want to do that," thought Art to himself. "Bill might get badly hurt."

"Oh, no, he wouldn't," the voice said. "All it would do would be to scare him a little."

The more Art thought about it, the better he liked the idea. If he could cut the rope just partly through, then it wouldn't break until Bill was swinging high into the tree.

"He'd sure go sailing," Art said to himself, laughing unpleasantly. He came out from behind the bush and stood in the twilight staring at the long rope hanging down from the branches.

"It wouldn't be at all hard to do," thought Art. "All I would need to do would be to get my pocket knife and shinny up the tree and cut the rope about halfway through. That's a honey of an idea; it really is!"

Turning, Art went whistling up the street.

An Unexpected Conversation

A S ART HURRIED HOME through the darkness, thinking over his new-found plan, he sort of felt happy for the first time since the hike last Saturday.

At last, he was going to be able to do something about his defeat and shame. Soon all the other boys would be laughing at Bill instead of him, he thought. Everybody would hear about Bill falling out of his swing and being frightened.

"Then they won't think Bill is so great," Art muttered to himself. "Then they'll find out what a baby he really is."

Swinging around the corner to the street where he lived, Art was surprised to see a strange car drawn up at the curb in front of his house. He slowed down and stopped whistling. First, he noticed that it was not a police car. He was a little relieved at that, but somehow, although he didn't think anybody could prove it, he knew perfectly well who it was that had stolen Mrs. O'Leary's lantern and had thrown it into the ditch. And he knew that sometimes the police came to see about things like that.

Moving cautiously forward he was right up to where the car was when suddenly the car door opened and out stepped a man

Art didn't recognize.

"Can you tell me where Art Smith lives?" asked the man. "It's supposed to be right along here somewhere, but I can't see the numbers on the houses."

When confronted with such an unexpected question from a stranger, Art's first idea was to say, "I dunno," and run away. But on second thought, he realized that that wouldn't help very much because the man would ask somebody else and he'd find Art's house and go in and talk to his mother and dad. Art didn't know what he might have come to tell him, but whatever it was, he didn't like the idea very well. He decided he had better talk to the man himself. "And anyway," Art thought, suddenly brightening a bit, "it might be something good instead of bad. Maybe the man wants to talk to me about joining his baseball team when I get bigger, or something like that."

So Art said, "Yeah, I know where he lives. It's right in there," and he pointed up the walk to his house. "As a matter of fact," he said warily, "I'm Art Smith."

"Well, well," said the man, thrusting out his hand, which Art could see from the light of the front room. "My name is Jim Grant and I live a few blocks away over on Elm Street. I've been wanting to meet you and talk with you."

"Yeah," said Art, suspiciously. "And why didn't you come in and ask for me instead of sitting there in the car in the darkness?"

The man laughed. "Well, as a matter of fact, I haven't been sitting there very long, but I was talking to Somebody about you a few minutes before trying to find you."

Art had heard of telephones in cars and he had seen two-way radios in taxicabs.

"To whom were you talking?" he wanted to know, suddenly interested, and then fear gripped him again. "Say, mister, you're not a policeman, are you?" he asked. "Squad cars have those two-way radios in them, don't they?"

"Yes, I think all of them do now," said the man. "But I'm not a policeman."

"Oh," said Art, relieved, "then to whom were you talking anyway?"

"I was talking to my heavenly Father," said the man. "I was talking to Him about you."

"You mean God?" asked Art. "You were talking to God about me?" He stared through the darkness at this strange man. "What were you talking about?" he demanded.

"Well," said the man, suddenly a little bit uncomfortable, "my name is Mr. Grant and I'm a new Sunday school teacher over at the Elm Street Church where I understand you used to attend."

"I've been there only once," Art said.

"Well," the man continued, "I've been planning for weeks to come over and invite you back again. And for one reason or another I never got to it and then yesterday I thought I—I—uh, I heard about your trip on Saturday and I—uh—thought you were in a little bit of trouble over it and that made me make up my mind to come over here tonight and talk to you, no matter what happened. So here I am."

Art was too surprised to be angry at Mr. Grant for talking about the trip last Saturday, and it fascinated him to think that somebody had been sitting there talking to Somebody in Heaven about him. It was the first time in his life that he had even known of anyone praying for him.

"And what did God say?" he asked eagerly.

"Well," said Mr. Grant, "I was just asking Him to help me have a nice talk with you and to help me tell you about how much God loves you."

"God loves me?" Art asked. "Say, I'll tell you what—I think you got me mixed up with Bill Baker. He's the guy that saved everybody from falling over the cliff. He lives over on the next block."

"God doesn't love us because we rescue people," Mr. Grant said. "He loves us anyway."

Art had never had very much love. At home there was nothing but quarreling and anger, and deep down in his heart he knew quite well that his leadership at school had not been because the boys liked him, but because he bullied them. And so when Mr. Grant talked to him about God loving him, he was interested.

"How do you know God loves me?" asked Art. "Did He tell you that when you were sitting there talking to Him?"

"No," said Mr. Grant. "He tells me that in this Book that I have here in my pocket. Here, come on in the car and sit down and we can read some of it under the flashlight."

And there as they sat in the dim light of the car reading the Bible, Mr. Grant told Art some things he had been wondering about for so long. He explained to him that Jesus Christ was God's Son and that God had sent Him to die for the sins of the world. And when He died there on the cross, Mr. Grant explained, it wasn't for His own sins, because He had never sinned at all. It was for the sins of all those who want to be included and forgiven. It was the old, old story that has been told for hundreds of years, a true story of God's great love, but it was the first time that Art had heard it with any completeness. He listened intently and read the verses carefully that Mr. Grant pointed out to him. He didn't understand a lot of them, but Mr. Grant explained them.

"Do you mean," Art asked at last, "that it's up to me whether I want to get to Heaven or not? I can be the one to decide? He wants me to come and, if I am truly sorry for my sins, all I have to do is ask Him to forgive my sins?"

"Yes," said Mr. Grant, "that's exactly it."

Art had a very strange feeling as he read the verses and heard Mr. Grant explaining them. He wanted to have Jesus for his Friend, and he wanted to go to Heaven when he died; but the thing that he kept thinking about was the plan he had to get even with Bill. And although he didn't know very much about such things, he seemed to know without anyone saying so that if he asked Jesus to forgive him and be his Saviour, he would have to give up his revenge. "Wouldn't you like to ask God to forgive you, and be your Saviour even tonight?" asked Mr. Grant seriously as they had finished reading together. "Now that you know these things, it's important that you decide and act. No one knows what tomorrow may bring."

Art didn't know that his answer to Mr. Grant's question was going to make that night one of the most serious in his whole life. What happened the next day would never have happened if he had repented and found Jesus as his Saviour right there while he was talking to Mr. Grant.

"Yes, I can see it's important," said Art, "but there's something I want to think about for a while first."

"Well," said Mr. Grant, "I don't want to press you too much. But I'm certainly going to pray for you, and I sure would like to have you come to our Sunday school next Sunday. How about it?"

Then Art's face darkened and an angry frown clouded it. "Is Bill Baker in the Sunday school class?" he demanded.

"Why, yes, he is," said Mr. Grant, "but I am sure he's not bearing any grudge about last Saturday. Just forget about it and come on to the class."

"No, thanks," said Art. "I guess I won't. And anyway, I've got to go in now. So long." And before Mr. Grant had time to say another word Art had opened the door and was gone.

Mr. Grant drove off, praying as he drove.

Art went upstairs to bed. He felt worse than he could ever remember feeling before. Some of the words Mr. Grant had shown him in the Bible kept calling to him. "My sheep hear my voice," Mr. Grant had said, reading the words of Jesus, "and they follow me." At least it was something like that. And Jesus wanted Art to be His friend, Mr. Grant had said. But Art had told Him "No"; not till he got back at Bill. Poor, foolish Art. Finally, he went to sleep, knowing full well that he had turned down the Shepherd's great invitation.

The Accident

IT WAS WEDNESDAY EVENING, two days later, before Art found the chance he had been waiting for—the chance to carry out his evil plan. His mother and dad had gone out for the evening, and Betty was already asleep. Quietly he sneaked out the back door into the dark night, dark except for the small moon that was hanging low in the sky. There was a coldness in the air that made Art shiver a little as he walked across the bridge and went the two short blocks to Bill's house. Walking cautiously up the driveway through the darkness, he found his way to the rear door of the garage, which was unlocked as he expected it to be.

Carefully covering his flashlight with his hand so that only a tiny ray could come through his fingers, he quickly found a stepladder. That was a relief because if none had been there, Art would have had to go back and get his dad's and drag it along the streets and sidewalks, and he thought that it might seem a little strange to anyone who might be walking by. They might even call the police. So Art was happy that he found one in Dr. Baker's garage.

Carefully and slowly, he moved the stepladder down from the wall and back out of the garage, dragging it behind him. Once the kitchen door opened and he froze in his tracks, terrified at the possibility of being discovered, but it was only Bill's mother putting something on the back porch and the door soon closed as she went back in. Then, carrying the heavy stepladder quickly across the gravel drive, he dragged it the rest of the way across the lawn to the tree where the swing was. The ladder was heavy and it was not an easy job to get it standing up against the tree, but at last it was there. Feeling in his pocket to be sure that his knife was ready, he climbed up and stepped out onto the branch where the ropes were tied.

Then quickly opening his knife, he sawed away at the top of the rope until most of it was cut, leaving only a small strand holding the swing. And that was all. The terrible deed was done. Now when anyone sat quietly on the swing nothing would happen; not until the person was swinging high, and then the rope would break and throw him across the lawn. "Bill should have a fine swing tomorrow night," Art thought, and grinned. "I guess I'll come and see the fun."

And then sliding the knife safely back into his pocket, he quickly came down, dragged the ladder back over the dry lawn, carried it across the driveway and silently moved it into the garage. He retreated carefully to the street and was soon whistling merrily as he ran home and upstairs to bed.

All that night, strange to say, Art slept soundly. When he woke up the next morning, he had a strange feeling that it was going to be a very exciting day, but for a few moments he couldn't remember why. And then his spirits rose as he realized that this was the day when he was going to get even with Bill. One thing was sure; he wanted to be there when the swing broke. He wanted to be able to tell the other boys about it in vivid detail. He could already see the surprised look on Bill's face as he went sailing over the lawn. Then tomorrow at school he would ask Bill about it and make fun of him and tell the other boys how clever he had been in fixing the swing so that Bill would have such a thrilling ride!

All that day at school Art kept looking at Bill and smiling a little to himself. Bill thought he was so smart, did he? Well, tonight he was going to have a surprise; then everyone would find out how brave Bill was. This was going to be fun! Art could hardly eat his supper that night because he was so excited and anxious to get over to Bill's yard.

"What's the matter with you?" his mother finally asked. "Are you sick?"

"Nope," Art said. "I'm just not hungry. Can I be excused, please?"

"Did you say 'please'?" his father asked. "Now I know you're sick. The last time you said 'please' was when you were just learning to talk."

"You're excused," his mother said hastily, fearing a quarrel was on the way.

Art rushed out of the house and over to Bill's. Then he walked slowly along as though he just happened to be going by. No one was in sight so he crossed the street and started cautiously up the Bakers' driveway until he came to a thick bush. He crawled quickly into the middle of it where he sat quietly waiting.

Supper that night at Bill's house was even more fun than usual. Everyone was feeling jolly and playful. Bill told riddles he had heard at school, and Dad and Mother and Josie tried to figure them out. Some were riddles that Josie's dad had told when he was a boy in school, but he pretended that he couldn't possibly figure out the answer, though Bill suspected that he knew.

"Why did the little boy throw the butter out the window?" asked Bill. And when nobody knew the answer (except Josie, and Bill wouldn't let her tell) he shouted happily, "Because he wanted to see the butterfly."

"I know one too," said Josie. "What word should always be pronounced wrong?"

"I give up," Dad said finally.

"I do too," said Mother.

"The word is 'wrong,' " said Josie brightly.

At their family devotions that night they read together the Twenty-third Psalm and talked about it and spoke of the loving Shepherd who cares for His sheep, even the tiniest lamb. And after they had prayed Josie said, "Daddy, will you push us high in the swing tonight before we get ready for bed? I want to see if I can touch the branches again."

"Aw, that's easy to do," said Bill. "I can do that every time."

"Well, you and Dad go out and have your swing," said Mother. "Josie and I will come out in a few minutes after we've cleared away the dishes from the table."

Bill and his dad went outside laughing and chattering together, happy because Dad could be home this evening when so often he was kept away.

That was the one big trouble with being a doctor, Bill's dad had so often said. "I hate being away from the children so much; but the Lord called me to be a doctor, so that's what I'm going to do."

On the evenings when Dr. Baker could be home, the family made the most of the occasion. And tonight was one of those happy evenings together which Bill and his dad were enjoying thoroughly.

"How high do you want to go?" Bill's dad asked. "As high as I can push?"

"Yes," said Bill, "just as high as you can make it go."

"O.K.," said Daddy, "here goes!" Then with a mighty heave, Bill's dad started him off. Higher and higher he went until the swing with Bill on it was heaving and jerking against the rope. Back again and up again he went. Higher and higher. Bill's dad had to jump now to catch hold of Bill and pull him to make the swing go higher still. Up and up Bill sailed.

And then, it happened.

The rope broke. Bill was almost lost in the branches when suddenly he felt himself tumbling out and down. There was a terrific thud as he, hit the ground. A sharp pain in his neck, and then blackness.

Mrs. Baker and Josie were just beginning to wash the dishes when they heard a shout from Bill's dad and rushed outside to see what the matter was. Dr. Baker was bending over Bill, crumpled against the low stone wall at the side of the yard.

"Oh, Daddy, what has happened?" cried Josie.

"The swing broke," said her father, white-faced with despair. "It looks like Bill has been badly hurt." Feeling Bill's neck carefully with his practiced fingers, Dr. Baker covered his own face with his hands.

"Oh, God," he prayed, "please help us now." Then looking up he said softly, "You'd better call an ambulance. We'll have to get this boy to the hospital in a hurry."

The ambulance didn't come at once, of course. While they were waiting, Dr. Baker did all that he could, and then there was nothing else they could do except just sit there in the yard, waiting with terror in their hearts.

Bill's dad said quietly, "Yea, though I walk through the valley of the shadow of death, I fear no evil, for thou art with me."

Then he prayed aloud, "Dear Lord Jesus, take care of Your little lamb tonight. Bill needs Your help, and we need it. In Jesus' name. Amen."

And then in the distance they heard the moaning of the siren of the ambulance as it came down the street and stopped in front of the house. Two young men jumped out with a stretcher and soon Bill was in the ambulance with his dad. Then the siren was wailing again and they weregone.

The River Road

I T WAS A LONG time after the ambulance had gone and the dismal, lonely cry of the siren had disappeared in the distance before there emerged from the bush on the side of the lawn a boy who walked slowly away as though in a dream. His head hung low and his shoulders hunched forward. There was such despair in his heart as he had never known before. Stumbling and crying, Art disappeared into the darkness. Not knowing where else to go or what else to do, he found himself halfway home when he suddenly stopped, then whirled around and ran back toward Bill's house as fast as he could go.

As Art ran he tried to figure out how to do something that he now realized was very important and that he needed to do right away. For Art had suddenly thought of something. Even in his terror and despair in what he had done, Art had not lost his crafty cunning. He had to see that no one would ever find out that he had caused Bill's accident. If Bill died, no one must ever know that he had killed him. No one had seen him, but tomorrow someone would surely notice that the rope had been cut.

Art knew they would ask, "Who did this?" and there would surely be some who would answer, "I wonder if it could have been Art Smith? You know, the boy who said he was going to get even with Bill if it was the last thing he ever did." All the children who had been on the hike and Bill's father, too, had heard him say it. Art knew those were not words that Bill's father would forget. Yes, he was lost unless he went back and carried off the rope so that no one would ever know that it had been cut.

But how could he get rid of the rope? How could he get it down from the tree? If he could only get it down, he could take it away and burn it somewhere. Well, he would certainly try. Tomorrow people would wonder why the rope was gone, but no one would ever know that it broke because it had been cut halfway in two.

There, was no time to try to sneak the ladder out of the garage again. At any moment someone would be turning into the driveway with headlights bright against the tree where the swing lay. He must try to climb the tree without the ladder and quickly before someone came. Gripping the rough bark with his fingers and tennis shoes, he tried to climb. But it was no easy task to go up a tree. Again and again he slipped down after he had gone a few feet up and fell crashing to the ground. It seemed a hopeless job and as a matter of fact, it was. He stood there helplessly holding the rope in his hands when suddenly he heard a step behind him and Jerry's familiar voice said, "Hey, Art, is that you? Did you hear what happened to Bill? My mom heard the ambulance and came over to see what the trouble was and there was Bill lying on the ground, out cold as a stone. He hit the wall over there when the swing broke. What are you looking at?"

"Oh, nothing," said Art who was scared almost out of his wits at being discovered. "I was just looking at the end of the rope."

Jerry pulled out his flashlight and turned it on. Then he whistled. "Art," he exclaimed, "this rope has been cut partway through. That's why Bill fell. Somebody's tried to murder him."

"But who would want to hurt Bill?" asked Art.

"Say," Jerry exclaimed, "how come you're over here looking at the end of the rope? You're the only person in the whole school that would want to hurt Bill. You didn't cut the rope, did you? It would be just like you, though. I know how I can tell. Let me see your pocket knife."

Art dazedly obeyed and pulled his knife slowly out of his pocket.

"Open it up," commanded Jerry. "Yep, just as I thought. There are some strands of rope caught on the knife. You did it. A murderer, that's what you are!"

Snatching the knife from Art's hand, and taking it with him, Jerry suddenly turned and ran across the street to his house and slammed the door behind him.

Stunned by this sudden new disaster, Art sank down to the ground under the tree and sat there almost unconscious of anything that was going on around him. He knew that within minutes the story of his part in Bill's accident would be known throughout the neighborhood. Just what would happen next he dared not think. Would the police come and take him away? And even if they didn't, how could he ever go to school again and face the jeering of his playmates? "A murderer," Jerry had called him. Was Bill really dead? He couldn't erase the picture of him lying there against the wall with his face white, his head bent in such a strange way.

"I didn't mean to hurt him," he cried over and over again. "I just wanted to scare him. Oh, I shouldn't have done it! What shall I do now?"

While Art was sitting there it began to rain, and the wind began to move in the trees above him and somewhere in the distance he heard the crash of thunder and saw the lightning flash. A storm was coming and he must get home. Home? Where was home now? Would his mother and father let him come home? No, he didn't dare go there to face his father's terrible anger and his mother's crying.

He couldn't go home, but where else could he go? A boy of his age couldn't just go anywhere he wanted to. He would soon become hungry and there would be nothing to eat. He would soon be very tired and there would be no place to sleep. He was so tired now that he didn't know how to think very clearly. But one thing he did know, he couldn't stay here. At any moment someone would be coming to bring news from the hospital or to get Bill's mother and Josie.

Jumping up, he ran down the street; running across the bridge, he kept going at a steady dog trot through the rain and turned up the alley that led to the back door of his house. He would have at least a few minutes, he thought, before someone would telephone his father and mother. And in those few minutes he could get some things from his room and get out of the house again before going on, where he did not know. His dog began to bark as he opened the gate of the back yard and he whistled softly to him. The dog came rushing to him with tail wagging and little yips of joy, but Art roughly bade him to be silent and went on. He opened the back door softly and taking off his shoes tiptoed into the kitchen. It was dark, but hearing voices in the front room he tiptoed across the linoleum and stood listening behind the door. His parents were talking loudly, his father angry and his mother alarmed.

"But I haven't any idea where he went," Mrs. Smith was saying. "He left right after supper and hasn't been back since. There was an accident somewhere in the neighborhood because I heard the ambulance a while ago, and it may be that he went there to see what was happening. But it's so late and I do wish I knew where he was."

"So do I," said Mr. Smith, in a tone of voice that Art didn't like. "If I knew where he was I'd go and get that boy and I can assure you that he would be sorry about staying out this late. In fact, he's going to be sorry anyway as soon as I catch him when he comes back."

"Oh, Frank," Art's mother said, "he doesn't mean any harm. I hope nothing has happened to him."

"Well, if it hasn't, it's going to very soon," said her husband.

Art didn't wait to hear any more. Slipping up the back stairs, he made his way into his room, and quickly pulled down his raincoat and rain hat, pulled a flashlight and a heavy sweater out of his drawer. Then, hearing steps on the stairs, he snapped off the light and crawled under the bed. In a few moments the door of his room opened and his mother and father turned on the light and looked in.

"See," said his mother, "he's not here. I'm sure we would have heard him if he had come in while we were downstairs. Frank, I think we should call the police and tell them that he's missing."

"I sure don't know what to make of it," said his father, less angry now and more worried. "Yes, I suppose that's what we should do, call the police. But let's wait a little while longer and see if he doesn't come in.

Then they snapped out the light, closed the door and went away. He slipped downstairs again by the same way he had come. On the way through the kitchen he went over to the stove and took a handful of matches, thrusting them deep into his pocket. Already a half-formed idea had begun to grow in his confused mind. Putting his shoes back on and pushing Rover aside, he softly closed the gate and found himself back on the street.

The storm was worse now with the thunder rolling viciously overhead and the lightning flashing. A little figure whose heart was beating loudly was running wildly through the wind and rain. On and on Art went, turning left or right at each corner without slowing, as though sure where he was going. Soon he came to the River Road where the headlights of a car appeared in the distance and Art threw himself into a wet ditch at the side of the road and waited until the car had gone past.

Then picking himself up, he went on until he came to the place where the Trail went into the woods from the road, the very same spot where he and the children had gone the Saturday before on their hike. Somehow it seemed to Art now that it was years ago that there had been a hike and happy children with fun and songs along the Trail. Tonight there was no happiness, only despair. Tonight there was no light except the light of the sky's jagged flashing above him, with utter darkness in his soul. Pointing his flashlight here and there in the darkness where the trail began, he suddenly darted forward and picked up Mrs. O'Leary's lantern that he had left there at the end of the hike.

He pulled out the matches from his pocket, and finding an old board that was still dry underneath, he sheltered it and the lantern as best he could from the rain and the wind. After three or four tries, he succeeded in getting it lighted. Then putting his flashlight into his pocket as a reserve in case he needed it later, he started up the trail. He turned into the darkness of the forest. He would not come back. Somewhere up the trail there were the cliffs and there he would solve the problem that he could not think how to solve in any other way—the cliffs and the rocks a thousand feet below. How long would it take before they found him there? he wondered.

How long before his mother and dad would call the police, and the alarm would go out to look for him? They would never think of trying to find him on the Trail. Weeks, even months, might go by before they would ever know. Perhaps they never would. "But after all," Art said bitterly to himself, "they won't care. Not much anyway. Maybe Betty and Mother will cry a little, maybe even Dad will be sorry just a little when he gets over being angry."

Thinking of them, Art hesitated for just a moment along the path. Should he go back after all? Should he go home to his warm bed where he could sleep? Sleep? Yes, how wonderful it would be in bed, safe and snug while the storm roared outside. But he knew he could never return. Not after what he had done. They would not want him ever again, not any of them. And with tears streaming down his rain-drenched cheeks, crying as he ran, Art moved steadily onward toward the cliffs.

The Captive

O N AND ON ART went, moving steadily, almost as though he did not feel the great drops of water falling from the trees, did not see the bright flashes of lightning that lit up the forest, did not hear the roar of the thunder. Once somewhere nearby the lightning struck a tree with a terrific crack that sent it thundering to the ground.

But Art paid no attention. He saw and heard and he was afraid, but even fear was overpowered by the deadness of his heart within him and the cry of accusation that pressed him forward to do what he had decided.

It was little wonder that he did not hear the footsteps coming rapidly and heavily behind him, for he was not alone on the Trail that night. Another figure moved silently and steadily after him. Flashes of lightning lit the forest and if Art had turned just then, he would have seen an old woman with unsmiling, grim face, her hair wild and wet, her dress flapping grotesquely in the wind. Closer and closer she came to the boy ahead of her. Who was this strange person and what did she want? Was it perhaps some witch?

Still closer she came, her footsteps drowned out by the raging storm until she was only one step behind him. Her arm reached forward. Only when a heavy hand gripped Art's shoulders did he whirl about and at the same time tried desperately to duck away and shake off the viselike grip.

"Oh, no, you don't, my good fellow," said the woman. "I guess you'll not be going any farther with my lantern tonight. So it was you who stole it?" Looking up, Art found himself firmly in the grip of Mrs. O'Leary.

"Let me go, let me go! I've got to go on. I can't stay here. Let me go!" cried Art, desperate in his fear.

"Oh, no, you don't," Mrs. O'Leary said, and taking both his arms began shoving him back down the path toward her house. "Like as not you've stolen something else and are just now going to hide it, though a terrible night it is to be out and doing honest work like myself, let alone thieving and stealing. I saw your light ahead of me on the trail as I came up from the village and I said to myself, 'There's strange business afoot this night. Who but myself has business up this trail on such a night? And my business is only to get home out of the beastly storm. So along I came at double clip, and me with my bad heart, to see what it was and why. And sure enough, there was my lantern swinging along as nice as you could please. Well, I've fetched it back now and the thief as well."

Talking incessantly, the woman pushed him along through the driving rain. In a few minutes they were on the porch where Art had stolen the lantern, and in another moment, they were inside, out of the storm at last. Mrs. O'Leary locked the door again from the inside and put the key in her pocket.

"You'll not be leaving for a while, my lad," she said. "Not until we decide what is best to do with you. It's not for my lantern that we're worried, especially now that I have it back again; but I've a notion others are looking for you this night. Now what's your name?"

"I won't tell you," said Art defiantly.

"Won't tell me, is it?" she said. "Then there's the police whose business it is to find out the names of thieving boys."

"No, no, don't call the police," cried Art. "Please don't."

"No? If you've done no harm, then why not? The police it is unless you tell me your name, so I can call your father and mother and tell them their little black lamb has strayed through the storm to Mrs. O'Leary's house."

"Oh, no, please don't tell my dad," cried poor Art. "He doesn't know I took your lantern. Please don't tell him where I am."

"Well, my lad," said Mrs. O'Leary with a softer look at the frightened boy, "I don't plan to let you go until I find out why a boy your age is heading up the trail on a night like this. Have you someone else I can call?"

"Yes," said Art slowly, "please call Mr. Grant."

"And who might Mr. Grant be?" asked Mrs. O'Leary. "Maybe he's some companion in crime with you."

"Oh, no," said Art. "He isn't a criminal. He teaches my Sunday school class."

"Your Sunday school class, is it?" asked Mrs. O'Leary, surprised. "And I thought boys that went to Sunday school didn't steal lanterns from old ladies. What kind of Sunday school do you go to and what kind of a teacher is this Mr. Grant who teaches you to do things like that?"

"Well," said Art uneasily, "he didn't teach me things like that."

"Maybe you haven't been going long enough," said Mrs. O'Leary. "How long have you been going to Sunday school?"

"Oh, not very tong," said Art and his face began to get red.

"How long?" demanded the woman suspiciously.

"Well, really not long at all I guess," Art mumbled. "I guess I haven't started yet."

"So that's it," said Mrs. O'Leary triumphantly. "Mr. Grant is the teacher of the Sunday school class you've never been to. Well, I guess we can't blame Mr. Grant about my lantern then. What's his first name?" she added, as she went to the telephone on the wall and picked up the directory hanging there on a string. "We'll see what Mr. Grant thinks about these strange doings."

"I don't know what his first name is," Art said.

"Guess we can try them all then," said Mrs. O'Leary. "That's if more than one are listed—which there aren't," she added after carefully searching up and down the page. "Well, Mr. Grant, you're going to get a fine surprise now. And, if you're asleep, you probably won't thank me for waking you up. Well, folks have been mad at me before and I've lived through it. And besides," she added thoughtfully under her breath, "if he's a Sunday school teacher, he shouldn't get mad."

Lifting the receiver, Mrs. O'Leary waited patiently for the operator to answer, but there was no response to her signal. Impatiently she shook the receiver hook up and down, muttering to herself. "The line's down," she finally decided. "Not a whisper can I hear." Slamming the receiver onto the hook she turned and shook her finger at Art. "You're causing an old lady a lot of trouble," she said sharply. "You'll be staying here this night. Come along upstairs and help me make a bed for you to sleep in."

Mumbling and grumbling, she led the way upstairs and along a hall that was full of fearful shadows that grew and sank as the lantern swayed along in Mrs. O'Leary's capable hands. She opened a huge cupboard door and took out sheets and blankets and soon made the bed in one of the rooms, making it soft and smooth. "You'll not be sleeping in pajamas tonight," she said. "But no doubt your underwear will do. Good night now, and I'd advise you to say your prayers before you go to sleep."

Setting the lantern on a stand near the bed the woman softly closed the door behind her and turned the key, and Art found himself alone. Here at last was his chance to escape. While he was trying to figure out a way to escape with the storm still lashing outside, the tired boy crept into the huge bed and went off to sleep dreaming of a little black lamb lost in the storm and a Shepherd out on the trail looking for him through the long, long night.

The Hospital

BILL KNEW HE WAS dreaming, but somehow he couldn't seem to stay awake long enough to think about it very much. Just as he began to think, he would fall asleep again and dream. It was always the same dream. He dreamed that he was standing at the top of a tree. Somehow something had broken and he was falling, falling, falling. Suddenly out of the sky, a giant eagle came and he landed in the eagle's soft feathers and was carried away safely to the eagle's nest. He woke up just as he landed safely in the nest, and as he woke up he heard a strange roar and he finally realized it was the cry of sirens somewhere ahead of him in the night. "Somebody must be sick or hurt," he thought. "Lord Jesus, help them to get better".

Then he fell asleep again and was in the eagle's feathers high in the sky soaring about gloriously in the sunlight. No, it wasn't sunlight; it seemed too bright for that. The siren had stopped now. Instead he could hear the murmur of voices, and opening his eyes he saw his father bending over him looking into his eyes with a bright light. "Hi, Dad," Bill tried to say, "I guess I've been asleep." He looked around and saw that he was in a room just like the one his father had showed him at the hospital one day, where people were brought for operations. "Where am I, Dad?" he asked in a puzzled voice. "Why am I here?"

"Don't try to talk, Billy boy," said his father. "You were in the swing—remember? And then the swing broke and you fell and we brought you here to patch you up."

The doctor was talking cheerfully, but Bill could see that his face was white and strange.

"Did it hurt me very much?" Bill wanted to know. "I can't seem to move."

"We can't tell yet, Bill," said his dad. "Just go back to sleep and we'll talk about it more when you wake up."

And then a nurse was smiling down at Bill. She put a cloth over his nose that smelled strongly of ether. "Just take a breath of this and count one and then another breath and count two, and see if you can count up to ten," she was saying.

Bill took a deep breath of the ether and was soon back on the eagle's wings again. But the dream changed now and the eagle was hurt. It kept falling down through the sky, down and down, farther and farther, down toward the cliffs somewhere below. Bill, in his dream, clung to the eagle desperately. "O Lord Jesus," he cried, "please help me. I need Your help. Please save me." And when he prayed the eagle wasn't hurt any longer and he again woke up.

When he opened his eyes he was in a little room that he had never seen before, and he was all wrapped up in some kind of a hard blanket so that he couldn't move at all. He felt sick and his back hurt. Without meaning to, he started to cry.

Suddenly bending over him was his mother, smiling at him. "Hi, Bill," she said. "You have had a long nap!"

"Where am I, Mother?" he tried to say. But only a little whisper came out.

"Here in the hospital, Bill. You were hurt last night when the swing broke. Remember? So Daddy brought you to the hospital and he and some of the other doctors have put you in a cast so that you can't move while your back and neck get better."

Bill was too sick and tired and hurt to think about it much or even care. He lay there with his eyes closed and soon drifted off to sleep again.

That was the longest morning of his whole life, it seemed to him. His mother was there and that helped a lot. But he wanted so much to see his dad and talk to him.

When Bill asked his mother how long it would be before he could be home again and be able to go out and play, his mother just looked away. "Wait until Daddy comes," she said, "and talk to him about it." When she looked at him again there were tears in her eyes that she tried to brush away without his seeing them.

And then finally he heard his father's voice somewhere outside talking to someone. At last there he was beside him, beaming down at him.

"Well, Bill," said Daddy, "this is kind of a surprise, isn't it? I gave you a good push on the swing all right and swung you right into the hospital."

Bill smiled because he could see that his dad was trying to cheer him up and act jolly. "Dad," he asked, "how long will it be before I can get home and run around again?"

Suddenly Dr. Baker stopped smiling. "Bill," he said, "I've got two things to tell you, but first I want to remind you about the Twenty-third Psalm we read together last night. Do you remember how it says that the Lord is our Shepherd? That means that He loves us and takes care of us in the very best ways, and sometimes those ways may seem strange to us and we wonder why the Shepherd leads us in among the rocks and thorns. I think that's because there are greener pastures beyond and we have to go through the rocks to get to them."

"I think the Good Shepherd is leading you through the rocks and thorns because He loves you. He wants us to trust Him to do what is the very best. We'll trust the Good Shepherd together, Bill."

"Yes," said Bill, "we sure will. I guess I can stand this a while, but how long do you think it will be, Dad, before I'm O.K. again?"

Bill's daddy turned away and walked over to the window. When he came back his face was serious. "Bill," he said, "I don't know how long it will be. It might be six weeks, and it might be a year, and it might be always."

Bill stared at his father. "You mean I might never get well?"

he cried. "You mean I may never be able to walk again? Oh, Daddy, I couldn't stand it. I just couldn't!"

"Perhaps you won't have to, Bill," said his father gently. "Perhaps the Good Shepherd is going to ask you to come and live with Him."

A band of steel suddenly seemed to press against Bill's chest so he could hardly breathe, and an icy hand seemed to chill his heart. "You mean that—I might—die?" asked Bill, terrified.

His father gently took his hand and held it close in his. "It might be, Bill. I don't know yet and I don't want to scare you. But, Bill, you belong to the Lord Jesus, and if it should happen suddenly, well—I think you ought to know."

Then his father began to pray. "Lord Jesus," he said, "oh, help us now! Help Bill and me and Mother and Josie to know how much You love us."

And then because there didn't seem to be anything more to say, Bill's father said, "I'll be back soon, son, and remember, we're going to trust our Good Shepherd together."

He paused and stood for a minute at the door, then turned slowly and came back to Bill's bed. "Son," he said, "there is one thing you ought to know. I'm telling you everything at once, and maybe I shouldn't, but there is something you're going to have to do for someone else."

"What can I do for anybody?" cried Bill as the terrible news began to sink home.

"Poor little fellow," said Dr. Baker, almost to himself, "won't You help him? 'Though we walk through the valley of the shadow of death,' You said, 'we need not be afraid.' But we are afraid. Do help us."

"Bill," he said, "the thing you can do for somebody else is to forgive him. That swing didn't just break; the rope had been cut. Art cut it, and now he is gone. I don't know where. He ran away and nobody knows where he is. Bill, remember what our Lord Jesus said when He was on the cross, 'Father, forgive them, for they know not what they do.' And Bill, you'll have to forgive Art."

Bill's eyes blazed with furious anger. "I'll never forgive him," he sobbed, "even if you have! You don't care if I die or if I'm always going to have to lie in bed as long as I live, you've forgiven him."

Bill's father was crying too as he whispered, "Lord, he's such a little lamb to be tested so heavily."

Bill Wins the Battle

WHEN BILL WAS LEFT alone after his father had gone, he could do no more than lie there and cry. The news he had just heard would have staggered a strong man, and Bill was really a rather small boy. Was he really going to die? It was a lonely, terrifying thought to go away from Mother and Daddy and Josie—to go where? To Heaven, Daddy had said, to be with the Good Shepherd always.

"But I don't want to go to Heaven!" Bill cried furiously. "I want to be with Mother and Daddy and Josie. And how could He be a Good Shepherd if He let me get hurt like this? It isn't fair. Oh, it isn't fair!"

But Bill knew in his heart that it was fair. Daddy had read so often from the Bible nights after supper about the Lord Jesus and how much He loves His children. Once, Bill remembered, Daddy had said, "Jesus doesn't promise us that everything will always seem like it is turning out right. Sometimes troubles come. Sometimes Jesus takes away the troubles when we pray, and sometimes He lets them stay." Then Daddy told a story about some missionaries who had been killed by the people they had gone to help.

"Jesus hadn't forgotten about them," Daddy explained. "In fact He was right there with them all the time. He saw the spears and the knives coming toward them and could have put out His hand and stopped them, but He didn't. He let the missionaries be killed. He wanted them to come to Heaven and live with Him."

Then another time, Daddy had told about a missionary who was saved just as he was in great danger.

"We don't know why God saves some people from having trouble and why some people have lots of it," Daddy had said. "We only know that Jesus knows best. Whatever He lets happen to us is always good for us. So far," Daddy had added, "we haven't had very much trouble or sadness in our family. But if He sends us troubles, too, I hope we will keep on loving Jesus and trusting Him just the same."

Bill remembered these things as he lay there crying. "Sure, Daddy can say things like that," he said to himself bitterly, "but he doesn't have a broken back or whatever is the matter with me. Then he'd feel different about it." Down in his heart, though, Bill didn't believe what he was saying. He somehow felt that Daddy would find a way to be happy even if he had to go away and live in Heaven!

And then through his tears Bill suddenly laughed a little bit. It wasn't a very big laugh and it might have been a little bit hysterical. But, even so, it was really a laugh, because Bill had just thought of something. "Here we always talk about how nice it's going to be up there in Heaven," he said to himself, "and how pretty everything is and how great it's going to be there with Jesus. Then, just as soon as we get a chance to go, we don't want to! Maybe I don't really think that Heaven is half that nice."

"Well, do I or don't I?" thought Bill, and he stopped crying so that he could think about it. He liked to think about things and here was quite a big thing to think about.

"No," he finally decided, "I guess I haven't really believed in Jesus very much. I thought I did, but I guess I really didn't." And because Bill really did love Jesus quite a bit, he said, "I want to start trusting Him right now, no matter what happens."

And then, illogically, Bill began to cry again. "I don't want to die," he said again and again to himself. "It isn't fair and I don't want to stay in bed for years and years. I'd rather die than do that. I wish Art would die. I wish he would get hurt real bad and not get well again." Then he cried all the harder because he knew it was so wrong to think of Art like that.

And so all that morning Bill was fighting against the Good Shepherd, and Satan was making suggestions to him. "It isn't fair at all, Bill," Satan kept telling him. "God doesn't love you, or this wouldn't have happened."

And all the time the Good Shepherd was whispering, "Bill, I really do love you. And if I love you and have forgiven your sins, then I'm going to love you forever and ever, and take care of you so you'll always be happier than you've ever been before —well, why won't you trust Me now to do the best thing no matter what it is?"

And sometimes Bill would answer Yes, and sometimes he said No.

Bill woke up early a few mornings later, with a feeling of excitement. Something was going to happen today, but at first he couldn't remember what. Then suddenly it all came back to him—today was the day of the operation. Today Dr. Larson would be flying in from New York, and Daddy had told him Dr. Larson was the best surgeon he knew to take care of accidents like his. From his bed he could see the sunshine outside and hear the birds calling to one another. Then once he thought he heard a flock of geese honking as they flew south to their winter home. Just for a moment Bill felt frightened and lonely.

Mr. Grant had been there to see him yesterday and they had had a long, long talk. Mr. Grant had told Bill just what to do at times like this. "Just start talking to the Lord Jesus," Mr. Grant had said, "and He'll take the fright away."

So Bill closed his eyes again. "Dear Lord Jesus," he prayed, "I love You, and You love me even more. I'm sure now that I want to love You no matter what happens. Please make me well, but if that isn't Your plan, then help me to serve You while I'm sick. If You want me to come and live with You, then that's what I want too. Amen."

When Daddy and Mother arrived after breakfast they found him happy and cheerful.

"Hello, son," said Daddy.

"Hi, Daddy," said Bill, looking up from the bed where he lay swallowed up in bandages. "Hi, Mommy. Did Dr. Larson come yet?"

"Hello, Bill," said Mother and she came over and kissed him gently.

"Yes," said Daddy. "Dr. Larson is here and just about ready to operate."

"Good," said Bill. "Daddy, would you pray now that the Lord Jesus will help him to get me well again?"

So Daddy and Mother and Bill bowed their heads and Daddy prayed.

Then the nurses came to get Bill ready for the operating room, and soon he was rolling down the hall on a bed with big wheels on it and into the room where Daddy and Dr. Larson were waiting.

A Change of Plans

WHEN ART FINALLY WOKE up the next morning he knew he had been sleeping a long time. The storm was gone and the sun was shining brightly into his room. He couldn't quite remember at first just where he was, but in a moment all the terrible things that had happened the day before came crowding back into his mind. Jumping up, he rushed wildly to the door. More than anything else he wanted to escape, but the door was locked. Going to the window he found it would open, but he didn't dare jump.

Standing there he could see the brilliant beauty of the morning. The rain-drenched woods were clear and luxurious, the birds sang, and even the crickets were chirping their autumn chorus once more.

The smell of bacon and eggs and toast floated up to him from somewhere below and he heard people talking. There was Mrs. O'Leary's sharp voice and there was someone else. It was a man's voice but not talking loud enough to tell who it was.

Presently he heard footsteps on the stairs. Mumbling to herself in a sort of friendly way and trying to come quietly as her heavy steps creaked along the hall, Mrs. O'Leary arrived at his door. "Are you awake, lad?" she called gently.

"Yes," said Art dully.

Mrs. O'Leary turned the key and opened the door. She stood there holding his shirt and trousers neatly pressed, feeling quite pleased about something.

"Hurry and get your clothes on," she said. "I have a surprise for you downstairs. And breakfast is ready." And then she was gone.

He washed his face and hands carefully in the bathroom at the end of the hall before drying them on the huge white towel. Even so, he left a black mark on the towel and turned it over so that it wouldn't show. Then slowly and with dread as to who might be waiting for him, he went down the steps.

"She's probably called the police," Art thought. "They're waiting for me down there. That's why she's so happy."

Opening the door at the foot of the stairs he stepped slowly into the kitchen.

There sat Mr. Grant. "Well, good morning," said Mr. Grant gravely.

"Hello," said Art. He was red-faced with embarrassment. And then, because he didn't know what else to say, he said, "I guess the telephone must be working again."

"Works slick as a whistle," Mrs. O'Leary said, beaming at Mr. Grant and Art. "Why, I hardly had time to lift up the receiver to try to call Mr. Grant about an hour ago when the operator said to me, she says, 'Good morning.' And I says to her, 'Prettier morning I never did see. But it's a Mr. Grant I'm wanting to talk with and his telephone number is 1157.'

"'I'll ring it for you, says the operator, and sure enough, in another moment Mr. Grant is there to say hello."

" 'Hello,' I says to him. 'Mr. Grant, I want your help. I've a wee chick here I found last night along the trail and his name he wouldn't tell, but he says he's in your Sunday school class, if ever he should go to Sunday school."

" 'That would be Art Smith,' says Mr. Grant real quick like. 'He's in bad trouble here and I'll come along right now and see what's next to do.

"So here's Mr. Grant, Art my lad, and he's been cooking up a real grand plan to help you out if you'll only have sense enough to say you'll do it. Now, Mr. Grant, tell the lad about it and we can eat breakfast while we're discussin'."

As the woman finally finished what she had to say, Art walked slowly over to Mr. Grant. "How is Bill?" he asked fearfully. "Is he hurt real bad? Is he d—?" His voice trailed off into silence.

"He's in bad shape," Mr. Grant said. "No one seems to know how it will all come out."

"Are you going to take me to the police?" asked Art fearfully.

"No," said Mr. Grant, "I'm not. Dr. Baker thinks he will not phone the police. Now, Art, here's the plan. Your dad and mother seem very much upset about what happened, and I suggested to them and to Bill's dad that it would be best if you got away from our city for a few weeks. They think so, too. I have your clothes in my car at the foot of the trail and I'm ready now to take you to my brother-in-law's farm at Overdale, about a hundred miles south of here. He and his wife agreed to take care of you as long as you behave yourself, and I told them you would. Now, what about it?"

Art listened in silence as the plan unfolded. He was angry that his parents seemed to care so little. He was tremendously relieved that Bill's dad wasn't planning to turn him in to the police, and he was very grateful to Mr. Grant for helping. A great burden was lifted, and at least a little ray of hope came when someone was there to help him and tell him what to do.

"Oh, I'll go! I'll go and I'll be very good," cried Art, and the tears began running down his cheeks.

"All right, Art, it's a bargain," Mr. Grant said, and he put out his hand. Art took it and a little smile came to his face.

"Thank you for helping me, Mr. Grant," he said. "I didn't know what to do."

"It's all right," Mr. Grant said. "Now eat the breakfast Mrs. O'Leary has made for you and we'll be off. Tragedies can work together for good, and I hope this one does."

The New Home

WHEN ART WOKE UP the next morning he couldn't remember at first quite what had happened. He knew he wasn't at home, and he knew he was all right. But for a few moments, he couldn't remember the long trip to Overdale yesterday with Mr. Grant. And then it all came back to him in a rush. Yesterday morning when he woke up, he had been a frightened prisoner at Mrs. O'Leary's. Then Mr. Grant had brought him here in his car. And now today he was far away on a farm with Mr. and Mrs. Gordon. He was among friends too. Why, yesterday afternoon when he came, Mr. and Mrs. Gordon had smiled at him and had been glad to see him. Mrs. Gordon had even kissed him, and that had embarrassed him.

"Hi, Art," they had said. "We're glad you've come to visit us." They knew about what he had done to Bill too, because Mr. Grant had told them when he had telephoned to ask if Art could come. Yes, sir, they were his friends. Art hadn't had very many friends in all his life, so it made him feel good all over to think that Mr. and Mrs. Gordon liked him.

As he lay there in bed thinking about how nice it was to be so warm and cozy, he heard footsteps in the hall. The door opened and there was Mrs. Gordon, looking young and pretty.

"Just like my mother," thought Art, "except Mom always

looks so worried and Mrs. Gordon looks so kind and peaceful."

"Hi, Art," greeted Mrs. Gordon. "How would breakfast sound to you?"

"Fine," Art said. "I'm really hungry." And tumbling out of bed he quickly dressed and washed and went downstairs. Looking out the window, he could see a barn, some cows, and some ducks waddling along the road.

"Hello there, Art," greeted Mr. Gordon as he came in from the hen house with a bucket of eggs. "How does it feel to be a farmer instead of a city boy?"

"All right, I guess," said Art grinning. "But kind of hungry," he added, looking at the big bowl of cereal, and the hot cakes and eggs on the table.

"Good boy," said Mr. Gordon, "I'm a little hungry myself." Then Mrs. Gordon came and they all sat down. Art quietly waited for Mrs. Gordon to begin eating, but she didn't. Instead she closed her eyes and bowed her head. Looking at Mr. Gordon, Art saw him doing the same thing and Mr. Gordon started talking.

"Dear Lord," he said, "we thank You for this food and thank You for bringing Art safely to us. Bless him, we pray. In Jesus' name. Amen."

Art wriggled in embarrassment. "Mr. Gordon must be praying," he decided. He had never seen anyone pray before, except Bill and some people at Sunday school. And the worst of it was that Mr. Gordon was talking to God about him. He didn't like that very well. If he had thought at all about God during the last two days, it was with a vague, uneasy feeling. He rather hoped that God didn't know where he was. And here was Mr. Gordon talking to God about him, and God would look down and notice him sitting there.

But then Mrs. Gordon began to eat her cereal, and Art soon forgot everything else in the joy of eating good food.

That was a day that any city boy would always remember. After breakfast Mr. Gordon said, "Come on, Art, wouldn't you like to help me put up some alfalfa?" And out to the barn they went where Art saw Dollie and Georgia, the two big horses. Mr.

Gordon showed Art how to harness them and hitch them to the wagon and then, putting in pitchforks and a jug of water, Mr. Gordon hopped up into the wagon, Art after him, and spoke to the horses. Dollie and Georgia seemed to enjoy the beautiful morning almost as much as Art, and away they rattled up through the woods across the meadow and into the hayfield beyond. Art bounced and shook and almost rattled as the wagon bounced over the rough ground; but it was fun and when Mr. Gordon let Art hold the reins and drive the horses his joy was complete.

While Mr. Gordon and another man pitched the hay onto the wagon, Art scampered along looking for field mice under the piles of hay and shouted with delight as the fat little creatures ran back and forth looking for their homes after the men had lifted the hay off their heads.

Then came the wonderful ride on top of the load of hay as it lurched and creaked across the meadow and through the woods to the barn behind the house.

After lunch, Mr. Gordon said they would go fishing, and Mrs. Gordon decided to go along. Quickly packing the picnic basket, they walked back through the hayfield and through the woods. Coming out from the woods, they were suddenly on the shores of a large lake, stretching for a mile or so to the dark, woodsy shore on the other side.

"I didn't know you lived near a lake," exclaimed Art. "I thought it was just a farm."

"Well, it isn't just our lake," said Mr. Gordon, "but it's anyone's fishing, so let's go." Mr. Gordon led the way to a boat that was tied to a tree. ""Here we are, Art," he said. "Now let's each catch a big fish for supper."

They all got into the boat and Mr. Gordon rowed them out into the lake. Then he showed Art how to put the bait on the hook, and how to hold the fishing rod.

And sure enough, Art caught a fish. He had hardly dropped the hook over the side of the boat when he felt a tug and then the pole bent and swayed as the fish tried to get away. It was a big one, too, and as it tugged and struggled, Art squealed with excitement. Mr. Gordon helped him get it into the boat. "That's big enough for all of us," said Mrs. Gordon. "Now we won't need to catch any more!"

And Mr. Gordon said that if Art could catch a nice fish like that the first time he guessed he could too. But they fished and fished, and nothing more happened. Art felt very proud of his fish. He wished he could have it mounted and show everyone when got home.

Mrs. Gordon finally said it was time for supper, so Mr. Gordon and Art rowed the boat back to the shore. Mr. Gordon showed Art how to find wood and build a fire and soon had one burning merrily. Mrs. Gordon cooked the fish in a frying pan. It tasted so good that Art decided he was going to catch a fish every day.

They got back to the farm that night all tired and happy. After such an exciting day with a picnic on the beach and Art's fish cooked over the open fire, Mr. Gordon said, "Well, Art, how do you like your new home?"

"Oh, it's really great!" said Art, with his eyes sparkling.

"Fine," said Mr. Gordon. "Would you like to join us now in our evening prayers, before going to bed? Every night we read the Bible together and talk to God about the day He has given us."

"Oh, O.K.," said Art, since there was nothing else to say. And anyway, it sounded like a good idea. "If evening prayers are as good as the rest of the day has been, they ought to be all right," Art thought.

So Mr. Gordon took three hymn books and three Bibles from the library shelf and passed them around. Mrs. Gordon suggested that they sing "What a Friend We Have in Jesus." She sat down at the piano and softly played it through once so that Art could get an idea of how it sounded. Sitting there in the warm summer evening, he read the words as she played the tune. Art became a little sad as he sat there. How he wished he had a home like this one! Everyone was so happy.

"What a Friend we have in Jesus," the song said. Art wondered what it would be like to have Jesus for his Friend. It must be awfully nice, he decided.

They all sang, Art adding his voice as best he could:

What a Friend we have in Jesus,
All our sins and griefs to bear,
What a privilege to carry,
Everything to God in prayer!

"Oh," thought Art, "if only I could talk to someone about my sins. This song says I can tell Jesus all about them. I wish I knew how."

They sang all three stanzas and then Mr. Gordon read from the Bible. Art didn't understand very much of it, and even though Mr. Gordon kept stopping and explaining, the words seemed too hard and didn't seem to make sense. There was something about "being justified" and Mr. Gordon said that meant "being declared righteous," but somehow that didn't seem to help much either.

Then Mr. Gordon suggested that they all kneel to pray. Art had never seen that done before and it seemed a little odd; still he supposed it must be all right or Mr. and Mrs. Gordon wouldn't be doing it and as he thought about it, it did seem the right thing to do. In a play at school, he remembered that all the servants bowed and got on their knees when they talked to the king, and after all, God was greater than any king.

What surprised him most of all was what Mr. Gordon said to God. He talked to God just as though He was right there in the room listening. Art had always thought of God as being a long way off in Heaven.

Mr. Gordon seemed to think that God had been with them all that day. Art hadn't realized that, or it would have frightened him. He didn't like to think of God watching him. He knew what God would be thinking about him and suspected it wouldn't be good.

Mr. Gordon seemed glad to talk to God. He thanked Him for the nice day they had had together and for bringing Art to them. He asked God to bless Art's mother and father. Then he prayed for Bill. "And, dear Lord, we are all of us sorry for what happened. Please take care of Bill in whatever way is best, and please help Art to learn more about Thee. In Jesus' name. Amen."

Art didn't say much after the prayer was finished and they got up from their knees. How he wished he could talk to God! God was a Friend of boys like Bill and kind men like Mr. Gordon and Mr. Grant, but Art thought He wouldn't have much to do with boys like him.

That night as he lay in bed thinking, before slipping off to sleep, he cried a little, wishing he could have God as his Friend instead of his Enemy. But there was no use thinking about it, so he brushed the tears away and let himself drift off to sleep.

The Expedition

ART SPENT HIS DAYTIME hours learning all about the farm. He learned to feed the horses and care for the chickens and ducks, to ride Dollie down to the mailbox, and to swim and fish. He enjoyed every minute of it.

One day he wanted to go exploring. "Mrs. Gordon," he asked, "could I have a lunch to take with me and go up the mountain behind the hayfield and explore?"

"Well," Mrs. Gordon said, "I should think that would be all right, except that you might get lost. Still, if you do, I guess it would not be too serious. There are farms all around the mountains and if you can't find the right one, you can telephone us. I wish we had some other boy who could go with you. Let me see if the Jones' boy down the road would like to go."

"I think I'll be all right by myself," Art said quickly. "I'd rather go alone."

Mrs. Gordon looked at Art tenderly. She had grown to love this lonesome boy who always seemed happiest by himself. Once he had asked her about Bill. When she replied that he had had his operation and that it was still too early to know what the outcome would be, he seemed satisfied with her answer and then wandered off by himself into the woods, for it was a heavy burden always on Art's mind, and there was no one to help him carry it. Mrs. Gordon understood his desire to be alone and away from people who might ask him questions that he did not want to answer, questions about why he had come to stay with the Gordons, and questions about Bill.

Soon Mrs. Gordon had a big lunch neatly packed in a box. She helped Art tie the box firmly on his back so it would be out of his way. He tied a bottle of water to his belt and went off happily, anxious to discover gold and hidden caves. Away up near the top of the mountain, Mrs. Gordon had told him there was an old cabin built long ago by a man who had lived there alone for years and years. There were strange stories about him, she had said, and some folks thought he had left a lot of gold hidden there in his cabin or in the woods nearby. But no one could find it after he died.

"But you might want to explore around up there," Mrs. Gordon had said. "And besides," she said with a twinkle in her eye, "Mrs. Jones down the road says the old place is haunted. She says she sees lights up there sometimes at night."

Art grew excited. "Oh, boy! There's probably a robber band up there looking for the treasure. I'd better be real careful."

There was no trail up the mountain from the Gordons' farm, so Art had to make his way slowly through the fields and meadows that crept close to the wood-clad top. It was a cool, crisp morning, and the squirrels were jabbering at him loudly as he passed below the trees where they were gathering nuts for the winter ahead.

Once he saw a porcupine ahead trying to hide behind a log. Bruno, the Gordons' dog, ran after it, barking furiously. He shouted at Bruno to come away, but Bruno wouldn't listen and ran after the porcupine. In a moment the dog came out, yipping with pain, his mouth filled with porcupine quills. Art finally got him quieted down and began the painful process of pulling them out one by one. Then he sent the dog home, where he seemed quite willing to go.

Pushing on, Art reached the edge of the deep woods near the top of the mountain and stood for a while looking down at the farmhouse far below and the lake beyond. It was almost time to eat his lunch, but he was too near the top not to want to find the old cabin first.

He turned into the woods and worked his way steadily upward to the trees, until he reached the flat and rocky top where no trees could grow. It was a beautiful sight. He could look far down on either side of the mountain to the farms in the valleys below. The top was flat and rocky, and just beyond him was the log cabin.

Art thought of the gold that was buried there somewhere and he decided it was a good idea to find it before lunch if he could. Stepping into the clearing he walked over to the cabin, stepped carefully over the tumbledown porch, across the broken boards, and pushed open the door.

A pleasant-looking woman was sitting there eating her lunch!

"Well, hello there," she said as Art stared at her in amazement. She certainly didn't look like the ghost of the old hermit and didn't look like a robber chief either. She just looked like someone quite nice and friendly.

"Oh," said Art. "I'm sorry! I didn't know you were here."

"That's because I eat quietly!" said the lady. "My mother taught me that many years ago while I was a little girl. Would you have some lunch? I'm just eating shredded wheat and milk with bananas on it. Do you like that kind of meal?"

"I sure do," said Art enthusiastically. "But I have some great sandwiches with me that Mrs. Gordon made for me."

"Fine," said the woman. "Sit down and we can get acquainted. I'm Ruth Bentley—the children around here call me Aunt Ruth. I live down by the lake and I bought this place last month and I come up here to paint pictures. Now, who are you?"

"I'm Art Smith," said Art. "I live with Mr. and Mrs. Gordon on a farm on the other side of the mountain. I came exploring to find the gold the old hermit hid who used to live here."

"Well, well," said Aunt Ruth, "I do hope you find it. Now suppose we eat. Do you want to ask the blessing or shall I? Or don't you ask the blessing at your house?" she asked.

"Mr. and Mrs. Gordon do," said Art, "but God doesn't know

much about me. I mean," he added hastily, "I'm not a friend of His very much."

"I see," said Aunt Ruth. "Well, then I'll ask it."

So they bowed their heads and Aunt Ruth prayed, "O Father, thank You for this good food. Now here is a boy who isn't Your friend, he says, and I think he'd like to be. Please tell him how he can be. In Jesus' name. Amen."

Art was surprised. He knew very well that he couldn't be God's friend because of what he had done to Bill. But then he realized that of course Aunt Ruth didn't know about that.

They had a pleasant lunch and then Aunt Ruth said that she wanted to do some painting and suggested to Art that he come along. "Paint the cabin?" asked Art.

"No," said Aunt Ruth. "Paint a picture of what we can see from the top of the rocks."

Aunt Ruth got a box of paints and the canvas she was going to paint the picture on and a frame to hold the cloth tight. They went up to the top of the mountain to the lookout point, and Aunt Ruth was soon painting a picture of the lake far below them. Art watched with interest as the blue of the lake and the dark green of the trees began to appear on the canvas. Seeing his interest, Aunt Ruth told him where to look in the cabin for another canvas, and soon Art found himself trying to paint a picture of the cabin. It wasn't a very good picture, but Aunt Ruth said that for the first one it wasn't bad at all. That made Art feel very happy. He liked Aunt Ruth. She seemed so friendly.

So when she quietly asked him, after they had painted quite a long time, about his home and his family, he found himself pouring out the long, long story about Bill and the hike and the swing. And when he had finished he added, "So now you see why I can't have Jesus for my Friend."

Aunt Ruth listened in silence till Art had finished his story. Absorbed in his misery, he sat staring down at the lake while she quietly went on painting for quite a long while.

Finally she said, "Art, Jesus wants to be your Friend, even if you did hurt Bill so badly. I want to tell you a true story.

"It's a story about someone who did something terrible, but

God forgave and loved that person anyway. Would you like to hear it?" "Oh, yes," Art said, "1 think I would!"

And this was Aunt Ruth's story.

"It was long ago," she said, "when I was a little girl. I had a lamb whose name was Isabelle. Isabelle used to jump and play with me when I took her walking in the meadow near my home. We had lots of fun together and used to chase each other up and down and around and around.

"I had a little brother four years old whose name was Melvin. Melvin loved to run and jump and play with us too. He was a good little boy and we all loved him very much. I had a nice sister, named Arlene. We often used to go with the other children from the nearby farms down by the big sand hill there on the lakeshore where I am pointing. On hot summer afternoons, we would build castles and forts in the sand. It was such fun.

"Sometimes our mothers would let us go swimming, or wading in the shallow water. I could swim so I could take care of Melvin.

"Of course, our mother couldn't always go with us, and because I was the oldest I was responsible for Melvin. I liked that because it made me feel big and grown up.

"Sometimes I took my lamb Isabelle, leading her along by a rope, and tied her to a tree where she could nibble the grass while I played on the sand and swam. They were happy days.

"One day, though, something happened that I can hardly tell about because it was so dreadful. Mother had said good-by as Melvin and I ran down to get Isabelle from the pasture to take her with us.

"I know you'll be careful, Ruth, and take care of Melvin!"

"And so we went happily down to the lake, taking turns chasing Isabelle and watching her leap high in the air whenever we came near her and then scamper away down the road again with both of us after her.

"Several neighbor children were there too and we played forts. Mine was the biggest that afternoon and all the children admired it and thought it was very wonderful indeed. Melvin helped me build it, and I remember how proud he felt.

"After a while we all went swimming and wading, and when I was tired I went to find Isabelle and tied her to a different tree so she could have some fresh grass. Isabelle was glad to see me and I played with her, not realizing how long I stayed.

"Suddenly I noticed that it was very quiet. Startled, I looked down to where the children had been playing but they were all gone. I quickly ran back down to the beach to see where all the children were and why they had run away. I could see some of them up the road running home.

" 'Melvin, Melvin,' I cried after them. 'Wait for me.' But he didn't come. One of the children turned around and came slowly back but before she got to me I noticed Melvin's little sailor hat was floating out in the water. Then the awful realization came over me. Melvin had been wearing his hat while he was wading and somehow he had fallen into the deep water and drowned. The frightened children had all run away when they saw what had happened. The little neighbor girl, looking very white and scared, told me that they hadn't seen Melvin disappear but suddenly noticed his hat floating there, and knew then what must have happened. Melvin, my little brother, was dead, there somewhere under the water.

"I screamed and ran as fast as I could down the road toward the nearest farm house. The neighbor was already running toward me because his little boy had told him what had happened. Soon other men came and my father too, and they searched a long, long time. Finally one of them found Melvin and lifted out his poor little blue body. They didn't know very much then about artificial respiration, and they rolled him back and forth on a barrel back and forth, back and forth, trying to make him breathe again, but it was no use. Melvin was gone up to Heaven to be with the Good Shepherd who loves His little lambs.

"But I—I was left down there by the lake, screaming and crying because I knew it was my fault. My father came at last when nothing more could be done for Melvin and lifted me gently in his arms to take me home. But I only cried the more and struggled out of his arms and ran away into the field, wishing I could die. How could I go home to Mother when I had let little Melvin drown?

"And it was there, late that night, that Mother finally found me sleeping exhausted under a bush. 'My little Ruth,' she said, taking me in her arms. And as she sat there beside me, we cried together

" 'But now Melvin is safe up there in Jesus' arms,' Mother said at last, 'and we will trust our Saviour.'

" 'No, no!' I cried. 'It wasn't Jesus' fault, it was mine. I was playing with Isabelle instead of watching.'

" 'Yes,' said Mother gently. 'One of the children told me. This is something you will always bear as a weight in your heart. But we love you, Ruth, and now you must come back and be our little girl again.' And gently leading me by the hand she took me home and tucked me into bed.

"After they had laid Melvin in his grave, I could not be comforted, and for many days afterward I ate little, slept little, and cried much. Finally Mother called me to her and said, 'Ruth, it does no good to grieve more now. We miss little brother beyond words, but now we must go on without him.'

" 'But, Mother,' I cried, 'you can never forgive me! You must always hate me for what I have done.'

"But Mother said, 'No, Ruth. Do you remember the time your little lamb was naughty and stepped on your kitten and it died? Did you ever forgive it?'

" 'Yes,' I said, 'I forgave it the very next day.'

" 'And which did you love most?' Mother asked. 'Your naughty lamb who belonged to you, or your sister's lamb that was always very good?'

" 'Oh, I loved Isabelle best,' I sobbed. 'Because she's mine.'

" 'Just so,' my mother told me, 'Daddy and I love you just as much as ever, because you are ours, no matter what you have done that was naughty and careless.'

"I put my arms around Mother and held her tightly, and from that moment I dried my tears. And though I grieved for my little brother, I knew that Mother and Daddy still loved me.

What I had done made no difference to their love. I was still their child, and they loved me."

Aunt Ruth ended her story and for a long time there was silence. Then Art said, "Do you think it is the same way with God? Do you think He will forgive even people who have done wrong things and love them anyway?"

"Yes, I do," said Aunt Ruth. "Jesus once said that He didn't come to help the good people, but He came to forgive sinners. Anyone who wants to be a child of God, no matter how wicked he has been, can ask God to forgive him and ask Jesus to be his Saviour, the One who died for all his sins. And God has never, never yet turned away anyone who truly seeks Him."

"You mean," asked Art eagerly, "that God would forgive me if I asked Him to, just like your mother forgave you?"

"Yes," said Aunt Ruth, "He would."

There was silence again, as Art sat there on the rock looking down at the lake where Melvin drowned. They didn't hate her when she was bad, he was saying over and over to himself. They loved her anyway. Maybe God loves me anyway—maybe after all He would be my Friend if I'd only ask Him.

Suddenly Art stood up. "I've got to be going," he told Aunt Ruth. "Mrs. Gordon will be worried if I don't get back soon."

"All right, Art," she said. "You come back some time and finish your picture, won't you?"

"Oh, that would be nice!" said Art. "When can I come?"

"Any time at all," said Aunt Ruth, and in a moment Art had said good-by and was gone.

That night after family prayers when Art was ready for bed, he got down on his knees by the side of his bed. "O God," he said slowly and earnestly, "this is Art Smith speaking. You probably don't know me, but I'm the boy that hurt Bill. I am sorry I did it and I am sorry about lots of other things too. Aunt Ruth says You love me and that You will forgive me if I ask You to. Oh, please, God, please do! And I want Jesus to be my Saviour because Mr. Grant says He died for my sins. And please help Bill. Good night now, God."

And Art got into bed and slept as he hadn't for many a night.

Home Again

WHEN BILL WOKE UP after his operation it was almost dark outside, and because the light in his room was not on it seemed dreary indeed. But in a moment he heard a familiar voice say, "Are you awake, son?" and his mother was bending over him and kissing him and the dreariness was suddenly gone.

"Don't try to wake up yet," she said. "Just go back to sleep for a little while." And Bill, content that his mother was there, slept again.

When next he wakened, Daddy was there talking quietly to Mother. "It looks mighty hopeful," he said and kissed her. Then he noticed that Bill was stirring, and seeing his eyes open he strode over to the bed. "Hi, Bill," he said. "So you're back again!"

Bill smiled weakly. "Hi, Daddy. I feel sort of sick to my stomach."

"Don't worry about that," Daddy said. "You look fine and Dr. Larson thinks you'll be on your feet again before you can say Jack Robinson—or at least in a few weeks."

"Oh, boy!" said Bill faintly. "Really? You mean I don't have to be in bed—all my life?"

"Hardly a chance," said Daddy.

Bill's face shone. "Oh, Daddy," he said, "aren't you glad? I wish you would thank the Lord Jesus for it right now."

"Fine," said Daddy. He and Mother stood close together, each holding one of Bill's hands, and Daddy prayed and thanked God for His mercies to Bill.

Then Daddy said that he and Mother ought to leave and let him sleep again for a while, so they kissed him good night. A few moments later he had drifted happily off again to sleep.

The days that followed were long ones for Bill. He couldn't sit up yet, so he couldn't read his books. Daddy brought him tapes of the children's programs that he liked, and that helped some. But most of the time he just had to lie there all alone. And yet he wasn't really all alone, for his Friend Jesus was there with him. Bill talked to Him sometimes and thought about Him until it seemed that He was right there in the room all the time—as of course He was! So Bill and the Lord Jesus became better friends than ever before.

As he grew stronger some of the children at school came to see him, and of course, Josie, his sister, and his dad and mother were often there. Josie was lots of fun. She made funny remarks, like Daddy did, that would make him laugh, or at least feel all smiley inside. The school children took turns bringing or sending games and library books and good things to eat. His teacher, Miss Edelman, came one day and he was glad to see her. He hadn't realized that she could be so full of fun.

"And now don't you worry about your school work," she said. "You'll make that up fast when you're up again." But Bill didn't want to get too far behind, so she told him where to start studying. The days went more quickly when he had more to do. He enjoyed catching up, especially in arithmetic and geography.

But one of the best times of all was when Mr. Grant came to see him. He really liked Mr. Grant. After they had talked about lots of things, Mr. Grant said, "Has anyone told you about Art, Bill?" Bill's heart missed a beat. He had wanted to ask but didn't quite dare. "No," he said. "What's he doing?"

"Well, he's moved," said Mr. Grant. "He's living on a farm with some relatives of mine and they say he is having a good time."

"Good," said Bill. "I've been praying for him every night before I go to sleep that he will become a Christian and love Jesus."

"Fine," said Mr. Grant, "you keep on praying and I will too. Maybe we'll be getting an answer to our prayers soon."

The great day finally came for Bill to go home. His father came into his room a few days before and said, "All right, Bill, let's see how you look standing up." And Bill walked! He wobbled and his father had to steady him, but he walked. And now, tonight, he was going to sleep in his very own bed at home.

That afternoon his mother had helped him put on his clothes and he had sat in a wheelchair while the nurse took him to the door. Then Dr. Baker had helped him into the car and they went off down the street—home again.

What a happy evening it was when Bill's family was together again! They laughed and talked and had fun, and then after supper, they sang a hymn of thanksgiving and Daddy read the Twenty-third Psalm again. Then they all prayed, thanking God for His kindness to them.

It was perhaps a week later that his father said, "Bill, I think it would be good for you to get out into the country for a while. You need to get outside more and have lots of things to do. Mr. Grant knows a farmer, Mr. Gordon, who would be glad to have you live on his farm. What do you think of the idea?"

"Living on a farm?" cried Bill. "That would be wonderful!" And then his face had a sudden frown on it as he realized that he wouldn't be at home. "How long would it be for?" he asked.

"I'd think a month anyway," said Daddy, "and Mother and Josie and I can come out on weekends."

"Well, that wouldn't be too hard," Bill decided. "I'd like to go."

"There's one other thing that I should tell you," Bill's daddy told him. "This farm of Mr. Gordon's is the place where Art is staying. Would that make any difference to you?"

Bill blushed a little. "Not to me," he said, "but I wonder if Art

87

would like it?"

"Mr. Gordon thinks it will be O.K.," his dad said. "He says Art will probably be glad to see you after the first embarrassment of meeting you again. As a matter of fact, it might be good for both of you."

Bill began to get excited. "We can have a lot of fun together. Art could show me how to do a lot of things he has already learned while he's been there. Oh, Daddy, I'd like it a lot!"

"Well, we'll see about it. This is Thursday," said his father. "How about planning to leave Saturday afternoon?"

The Meeting

THE SUN WAS SHINING brightly when Art woke up Saturday morning and he jumped out of bed excitedly. Today some visitors were coming, and Mr. and Mrs. Gordon wouldn't tell him who. "It's a surprise," Mr. Gordon said; "and I'm pretty sure you couldn't guess, so don't even try."

"Is it Mom and Daddy?" asked Art.

"No," said Mr. Gordon; "that is, not this time," he added hurriedly as he saw Art's disappointment. "But we'll see if we can't get them out here soon.

"Is it Mr. Grant, then?" asked Art hopefully.

"No," said Mr. Gordon. "Now, no more questions; you just wait and see."

Art hurried out to the barn to see if he could help feed the cows. Then it was time for breakfast. Art ate two fried eggs, a big bowl of oatmeal, some bacon and toast, milk and orange juice.

"That boy eats like a horse," said Mr. Gordon. "Maybe that's what comes from letting him feed the horses!"

"I think he's grown a couple of inches since he's been here," Mrs. Gordon said. "And growing boys like food, don't they, Art?"

"They sure do," said Art as Mrs. Gordon brought on a plate

of hot biscuits and honey, and Art helped himself to three of them.

After breakfast Art helped Mrs. Gordon fix up the guestroom and bring an extra bed into his room too. The mystery grew bigger and bigger as the morning went slowly by. Who was coming?

After lunch, Art was in his room when he heard a car on the gravel driveway outside. He ran downstairs and out on the front porch and there he stopped. His heart seemed to stop, too, as sickness and fear gripped him. He stood there, staring at the boy who was stepping out of the car. It was Bill: the boy he had tried to hurt; the boy he had almost killed. Bill, the boy who would hate Art the rest of his life for what he had done to him.

But even as Art watched in terror, a strange, wonderful thing happened. Bill looked all around as he stood there on the driveway looking for something. And then, as his eyes glanced up to the porch where Art stood, Bill saw Art standing there and smiled a big smile.

"Hi, Art," he called. "Look, I can walk!" And over he came to the porch and the two boys shook hands in their best grown-up fashion.

After that both boys broke loose and laughed and shouted as Art took Bill down to the barn to see the horses, then on a grand tour through the hen-houses, and to the pastures to see the sheep and cows; then to the pig pen and turkey house. Art and Bill returned to the refrigerator in the kitchen where Mrs. Gordon had put some of her best ice cream for the boys when they got hungry.

That night after supper, as the big family gathered for evening Bible reading and prayer, there was much joy and praising the Lord for His kindness in making Bill well again. Mr. Gordon suggested that each person should pray, although when he made the suggestion he looked at Art a little uneasily, afraid that Art might not want to.

But Art wasn't worried.

Mr. Gordon prayed first, then Bill's daddy and mother, then Bill. He was so used to praying for Art each evening that before he realized it he was saying, "God, . . . and please help Art become a Christian and learn to love You—." Then catching himself he stopped abruptly, not knowing quite what to do because he had suddenly realized that Art was listening! Art forgot that he was supposed to be praying silently and said out loud, "Oh, Bill, I am a Christian now. I asked Jesus to come into my heart one night last week!" And then he was embarrassed because it was prayer time and he wasn't supposed to be talking!

But Mr. Gordon said, "That's wonderful, Art! We're very glad." And Mr. Gordon prayed again and thanked God that Art had found a Friend who would always be with him.

And so the happy evening ended.

The Visit

T HE TWO BOYS SPENT happy days together, working and
playing, hiking, boating, fishing, and playing checkers after
supper in the dining room. Even going to a new school was fun
for Bill. The school was about a mile down the road, just far
enough for a nice walk after breakfast. The road ran through the
woods part of the way, and sometimes on their way home the
boys would pile up huge armfuls of leaves and build forts with
them.

And day by day Bill grew stronger. The pain that had been so
annoying when he was in the hospital was all gone now, and his
cheeks that were so white when he came home were becoming
fat and rosy.

One Thursday morning, a few weeks later, a letter came from
Bill's dad with the good news that Josie and Betty were coming
Friday night for a visit. They were coming alone. Dr. Baker was
going to take them down to the station right after school and see
that they got on the right train, and at 7:30 they would be at
Woodbridge, just seven miles from Mr. Gordon's farm. Mr.
Gordon and the boys would meet them with the station wagon,
and there would be one of Mrs. Gordon's wonderful farm
suppers ready for them when they got back.

Bill and Art could hardly wait for the next day to come. They made all kinds of plans—where to go and what to do. "I wish there would be school Saturday," Art said, "so that they could go to school with us and meet all our new friends and Miss Jones. She's a nice teacher."

"I don't wish there was school on Saturday!" Bill declared. "School's O.K., but not on Saturday."

"I don't really wish it," explained Art, "only it would be fun to have them see what a two-room country school is like."

"Maybe we can at least look through the window," Bill suggested, "if we go on a hike."

"Hey, I know what!" Art said, and began to look excited. "I know a good place to go. It's up on top of the mountain back of the house. We could take our lunches and all hike up there Saturday morning and come back in time for supper."

"What's up there?" asked Bill a little bit doubtfully. He felt fine, but he wasn't sure he'd like to climb a mountain.

"Well, for one thing," Art said, "there's an old log cabin where an old hermit buried a big treasure."

"Wow!" said Bill, his eyes widening. "How do you know?"

"Because Mrs. Gordon said that's what everybody thinks," said Art. "And besides it's supposed to be haunted—only it really isn't. People have seen lights up there at night, but I know why."

"Lights?" exclaimed Bill. "The place must really be haunted."

"Nope," said Art, "it's a mystery. You'll understand it all when we get there."

"Yikes, let's see if Josie and Betty would like to go," said Bill. "That sounds like lots of fun."

And so the boys planned for the big hike.

Even though they didn't think it ever would come, the next day finally arrived. As soon as school was out the boys hurried home.

Piling into the station wagon, they were soon on the way, with Mr. Gordon at the wheel. They sang songs as they were driving along, and most of the songs were hymns that Art was beginning to learn in Sunday school and at church. They arrived at the station just as the big yellow streamliner, with all its

93

windows brightly lighted, came rushing around the bend below the town and slowed down for the stop.

The boys ran up and down the platform, too excited to stand and watch, until Mr. Gordon asked them to stand still so they wouldn't be bumping into the people waiting to get on when the train stopped. A porter jumped down when the train finally stopped, and the first two people he helped off were Betty and Josie. The boys shouted to them and they waved, but couldn't run and jump even though they were all excited, too, because they had their suitcases to carry. The boys leaped in a circle around them and then remembering their duty, they grabbed the suitcases and ran with them to the car while Mr. Gordon greeted the girls and showed them where the station wagon was waiting. Everyone piled in, and in a few moments they were on their way, chattering happily, everyone trying to talk at once.

Everyone, that is, except Bill's sister, Josie. She was strangely silent.

It had been a hard trip for Josie. She hadn't wanted to come. When her father had asked her whether she would like to visit Bill, she squealed with delight because it had been five weeks since she had seen her brother, whom she loved very much. But when she remembered that Art was there too, her happiness left. She didn't want to see Art. She didn't want ever again to see this boy who had hurt her brother. She hated him.

And now, there in the station wagon while everyone else was talking happily, Josie sat in a corner, angry and silent.

She kept looking at Art and her mouth became hard and unfriendly. There he was, the boy who had almost killed her brother, laughing and jumping around and trying to act funny. She hated him! And there was Bill, acting as though he and Art were good friends. Bill ought to hate Art too, Josie thought fiercely, after what he had done, instead of having fun with him.

Fortunately Art didn't notice. He was too busy talking to his sister and asking questions about things that had happened at home while he was away.

Supper that night was full of fun too. Josie said not a word to Art, but to all the others she was happy and gay and told about all the things that had happened on the train ride; about the funny conductor who made faces at them when he went by. Once he even brought them ice-cream cones.

The girls had a message for Mr. and Mrs. Gordon. The message was from Josie's and Bill's father. The Bakers were planning to drive down to the farm the next evening.

That gave Bill a big idea. "I know what let's do. Daddy and Mother will have to talk so much at first with Mr. and Mrs. Gordon that they won't miss us, and we can have an overnight hike! We'll cook our supper at the top of the mountain, and the girls can sleep in the cabin and Art and I can sleep on mattresses made out of branches."

"Sleep in a haunted house?" asked Betty and Josie at the same time. "Well, I guess not!"

"You might like it better than you think," Art said mysteriously.

"Can we? Can we have an overnight hike?" the children begged Mrs. Gordon. "Please say 'yes'."

"Well," said Mr. Gordon as his wife looked inquiringly at him, "I think it would be all right if they want to. You can carry blankets on your backs and take what food you need, and there is a spring up there near the top where you can get water. Art and Bill can protect you from the ghosts, I guess!"

"I think Bill could," Josie said pointedly, "but I don't think Art could help much if one came around."

"Hey, sis, cut it out!" exclaimed Bill, and Mr. and Mrs. Gorden looked surprised. Art's face flushed red.

Josie mumbled something about being sorry and became silent again. The boys were surprised when they woke up the next morning and found that it was already seven o'clock.

It was, a beautiful day for a hike. The morning air was crisp and clear, and not too cold. The sky was blue overhead and the woods were full of brilliant colors, resting against a somber background of tall green fir trees and spruce. Rabbits ran across the path in front of them from time to time, and the dog took off after them with much loud yipping and yapping, but soon returned breathless, only to try again.

But Josie was not thinking of the beautiful morning as she walked along. Her heart was in a turmoil. "Why should Art be going on a hike with us?" she was asking herself. "Why should he be treated nice after what he did to Bill? He ought to be made to suffer. He hasn't any right to be with the rest of us." While these bitter thoughts were still in her mind, a Bible verse came popping into her mind, too.

"Hereby shall all men know that you are my disciples, if you love one another," the verse said. That means to love those who have hurt you, Josie. It means you are to be Art's friend. Not hate him, even though he hurt Bill so badly.

"I'll never be Art's friend!" Josie stormed to herself. "He's a bully and a coward and—and—a murderer."

Perhaps he was, Josie, a voice inside her seemed to say, but now he loves Jesus. Bill said so and all has changed. If you hate your brother, the love of Christ is not in you. If you hate Art you can't love Jesus.

"Yes, I can!" Josie said furiously. "Jesus wouldn't want me to forgive someone like Art."

Jesus' disciples said, "How often shall we forgive? Seven times?" Jesus said, "Truly I say, until seventy times seven." Lovest thou Me, Josie? Then feed My lambs. Help Art; don't try to hurt him.

"No!" cried Josie. "No, no, no!"

And right then in Josie's heart as she told God 'no', everything became dark, unhappy and afraid.

The others tried to laugh and sing and joke, but it wasn't easy while Josie was walking along in such sulky, sad silence. Only Bruno jumped and romped and ran and barked, not aware of the dark sweeping storm in a little girl's heart.

Somehow the morning slipped away, and just as the sun was reaching its noontime mark in the sky, and Bill had just said for the sixth time that he was getting rather hungry, they came out of the woods into the clearing that Art knew meant they were almost to the top. In a few moments they would be able to look down onto the cabin. Art let out a shout, and Bruno yelped in scared surprise and started running down the trail with his tail between his legs. Even Josie almost had to laugh, and the boys roared and clapped with delight when Bruno suddenly sat down on the trail to stop himself, bumped to a halt, and looked back with ears cocked to see why everyone was laughing. Seeing that everything seemed all right, he turned around and ran happily back to the children, his tail wagging, trying to act as though nothing had happened.

"We're almost there," said Art happily. "Just over the top we'll be able to see the cabin."

All morning Josie had felt miserable and unhappy.

No matter how much she tried, she couldn't seem to say anything nice to anybody. She knew how naughty she was being, but she couldn't seem to help it. She was frightened and worried. And the voice in her heart that she had tried not to listen to kept saying:

Are you a Christian, Josie? Really and truly? Or do you just say so because Bill and Mother and Daddy are?

"Of course, I am," Josie said to herself, almost crying.

If you love Me, keep My commandments, the voice said. This is My commandment, to love one another. But you hate Art. Are you a Christian, Josie?

At the top the children stood looking down over the lake. It was a beautiful spot. "Let's eat lunch here," Betty said, and all the others agreed.

"But first," Art suggested, "let's go down to the cabin because I want to show you something that lives there."

"Lives there! Is it a bear?" Bill asked in surprise.

"Probably a squirrel," Josie said peevishly.

"No," Art said, "it's something much nicer. Come on and I'll show you."

In a moment they were at the cabin door and he knocked. "Why are you knocking?" Josie asked. "Does someone live here? I thought you said it was haunted."

"But it's not," said a voice from inside. "Come in."

Josie and Betty were a little frightened, but Art opened the door and went in and the others followed. It was a cozy, warm kitchen they stepped into, bright and pleasant. And in the next room they could see a woman with a half-finished picture in front of her and a paint brush in her hand.

"Well, hello, Art," she said as they all came in. "I'm so glad you've come back for another visit. And your friends are welcome too."

Art introduced the other children.

Josie liked Aunt Ruth in a special sort of way right from the first meeting. "She's tops," she whispered to Betty. "She's nice. I hope I can be like that someday."

Dreams for Josie

A UNT RUTH MADE COCOA for the children's lunch and
they all ate together, sitting outside on the old porch. Aunt
Ruth kept them merry with her happy conversation.

After lunch all except Josie went off to look for hazelnuts,
because Aunt Ruth had said she had been planning to get some
and just couldn't get around to it.

Josie decided to stay with Aunt Ruth. As usual Aunt Ruth
decided to do some painting, and before long she was letting
Josie paint too. Josie's picture was of a pine tree standing near
the cabin. It was a tall, rugged tree, dark and somehow sad.
Josie was half surprised to see how well her picture began to
look.

"Art painted a very nice picture, too," said Aunt Ruth, "when
he was here last week."

"Yes," said Josie before she realized what she was saying,
"I'm sure Art's picture would be quite wonderful. He thinks he's
so smart. He ought to be in jail."

Aunt Ruth looked very much surprised and Josie felt very
uncomfortable. Aunt Ruth silently applied another stroke of
bright red to the autumn leaves she was painting.

"He's mean and hateful," said Josie. "And he hurt Bill very
badly. And now Bill has forgiven him, and Art hasn't tried to

make up for it or anything—as if he ever could."

"And Bill is right," said Aunt Ruth quietly. "That is God's way. We are to forgive those who do us harm instead of trying to pay them back and get even. When a person asks God to forgive him, Josie, does God say that first He will give that wicked person what he deserves, and pay him back?"

"No," said Josie stubbornly, "but it's different with Art; he ought to be hurt just as badly as Bill."

"Josie," said Aunt Ruth, "you don't really mean that, I hope. Have you ever sinned?"

"Of course," Josie said.

"And do you remember what the Bible says about one sin, Josie? That the wages of sin is death and Hell?"

"Yes," said Josie.

"And did God treat you as you deserved?" asked Aunt Ruth.

"No," Josie said. "He forgave my sins because Jesus died for them."

"And, Josie, doesn't God say that you must forgive others just as He has forgiven you?"

"Yes," Josie said, "but Art ought to be punished anyway."

Aunt Ruth didn't say anything for a little while and then she asked, "Josie, are you really a Christian? Some people say they are when they have never really been saved at all. They fool themselves. If you don't love Jesus enough to obey Him, then you don't love Him."

Josie was stunned. Of course she was a Christian! She had known about Jesus as far back as she could remember. The idea of Aunt Ruth asking a question like that? How dare she say such a thing?

Perhaps it was because of Aunt Ruth's question that Josie began suddenly to feel cold and shivery. Or, perhaps it was because the afternoon sun slipped behind the clouds and became tangled up and lost, and the wind began to blow, and there was a sudden hint of rain or snow.

"I'm cold, Aunt Ruth," she said. "Could I please go in the cabin?"

"Of course," said Aunt Ruth. "I'm beginning to shiver too,

but I would like to finish this part of the picture. I'll be there in a few minutes."

But being inside didn't seem to help Josie, even though it was warm there and the wind was kept out by the thick mud-chinked walls. She kept on shivering and when Aunt Ruth came in a few minutes later, she found Josie huddled in the corner near the stove with her heavy jacket buttoned tightly around her.

"Josie," Aunt Ruth exclaimed, "don't you feel well?"

"No," said Josie. She felt sick and miserable and began to cry.

It didn't take Aunt Ruth long to get Josie tucked into bed and she was asleep when the boys and Betty came pounding up the stairs and bursting into the cabin.

"Boy, is this ever going to be fun!" said Art. It's snowing hard." Sure enough, the clouds had become a thick gray ceiling and the wind had risen until the little cabin shook when the wind hit it. The wind moaned and sighed outside around the corner of the house, just beyond where Josie lay in troubled sleep. In her sleep she kept dreaming, but all her dreams were unhappy.

Sometimes it seemed to her that some little animal of the forest was crying in the wind and cold, but when she went to find it the crying drifted farther away. Try as she might, she could never quite reach and comfort the lost, hurt creature. And then in a distance she would see that someone was hitting something —she couldn't quite see what it was—hitting it again and again with a stick as it cried out its pitiful wail. In her dream she floundered angrily through the storm toward the person, crying out to stop hitting the little animal. Closer and closer she came until at last she could see that it was a little squirrel crying, only it was a strange little squirrel that had Art's face; it was a little girl who was so cruelly beating him. And when the little girl looked up at last, Josie gave a cry of terror in her sleep, for the girl was herself. She woke up when she cried out and Aunt Ruth was there bending over her.

"Are you all right, dear?" Aunt Ruth asked anxiously. "You were crying out in your sleep." She felt Aunt Ruth's cool hand on her hot forehead.

And then it was dark again and she seemed to be outside in the cruel storm, crying, and there was the cabin across the clearing, but she was too cold to go on and the wind was too strong. She lay there where she had fallen and a beautiful angel seemed to come, walking quietly toward her and picking her up, and carrying her to the cabin. And when she looked at the angel it was Art, who had found her and had come to help her. Then a voice from somewhere above her, she couldn't tell just where, said loudly, "This is the little girl who was hurting you. Leave her out in the wind and cold." She shivered, but the strong arms never faltered and soon she was inside, warm again and safe.

"He would," Josie said out loud. "I know he would."

"Would what, dear?" asked Aunt Ruth gently. "I couldn't quite hear what you were saying."

"Would help me even though I hated him," murmured Josie.

"Who would, Josie?" asked Aunt Ruth. "Are you talking about Jesus? Yes, He would, because He is so kind."

"Jesus is so kind, so kind to love me first before I even knew Him," Josie murmured and fell asleep again.

"Do you really love Jesus, Josie?" Aunt Ruth's voice sounded so clear in her dream and she was looking at her over her painting, and the sun was shining. Only it wasn't really. If Josie could have stayed awake, she would have seen out the little window that it was dark now and the snow blowing along the trail, piling up behind the logs, driving hard and white against the tree trunks, until they stood like white ghosts that creaked and rattled in the gale. But Josie saw the sun shine in her dream and Aunt Ruth, tender and anxious, was leaning over her. "Are you all right, Josie?" she asked.

"I hate him," Josie said. "He hurt Bill and I hate him."

"Josie, are you sure you are really a Christian?" That was what Aunt Ruth had asked her as they were painting that afternoon.

In the next room Josie heard the murmur of voices and realized she had been asleep and dreaming. Her mouth was dry and her head ached terribly. But the question Aunt Ruth had asked wouldn't go away.

"Am I a Christian?" Josie asked herself, and then with great effort, for she seemed to be falling asleep again, she said, "Jesus, I don't know whether I really have loved You. But I want to, and I don't want to hate anybody, not even Art. Thank You for loving me and for dying for my sins."

And then it was dark again.

"Art," she called, but no voice came from her lips. "Art, I don't hate you. You belong to Jesus, and so do Bill and I. I'm sorry." But he couldn't seem to hear her, walking ahead of her there on the path through the storm. "I want to tell him," Josie cried. "I want him to know."

"Know what, Josie?" asked Aunt Ruth anxiously as she came back into the room. But Josie didn't hear her because the storm had stopped, and she was out in the sunshine behind the cabin watching Aunt Ruth paint the pretty picture. That is why she seemed to smile a little as Aunt Ruth felt her hot forehead and then tiptoed back to the kitchen with a great fear stabbing at her heart.

Into the Night

AUNT RUTH CLOSED THE door quietly behind her and turned with a worried face to the three children who were sitting quietly in the kitchen.

"I'm afraid she is very sick," she said. "And I don't know what to do for her, since I don't know what's wrong, and don't have anything to give her."

They looked at each other helplessly and Art and Bill both said almost together, "We'd better ask God to help us."

"Yes," said Aunt Ruth, "we surely must. It's wonderful to know that He is here to help us and to tell us what to do."

So they all went down on their knees there in the cabin and asked God to help Josie.

"Oh, if only Daddy were here," Bill said, trying not to cry. "I wonder if we could run and get him?"

"No, Bill," Aunt Ruth said, "the storm is too bad and it's getting very cold. I don't think you could possibly get there tonight unless the storm stops. We'd find you somewhere frozen to death in the morning. No, we'll need to trust God to heal Josie. Perhaps she will begin to feel better soon."

They had supper then, and afterward, because there didn't seem to be anything else to do, the children made their beds on some newspapers on the floor, pulled their blankets tightly around them and lay listening to the winter's first storm roaring outside. Finally they fell into a fitful sleep after praying again that God would make Josie better.

Aunt Ruth, meanwhile, sat quietly by Josie's bed, praying and bathing her forehead with cool water. She had found a bottle of aspirin tablets and roused Josie enough to give her two of them. But it didn't seem to help. Aunt Ruth's face grew more and more drawn and helpless as the minutes ticked away and grew into hours. The child was not getting better and the storm was, if anything, worse. Josie was delirious now, talking wildly at times and then sinking into a deep sleep before rousing again to cry out something Aunt Ruth couldn't understand.

Perhaps it was when Josie cried out his name once that Art suddenly was wide-awake. How long he had slept he couldn't tell. For a moment he felt warm and cozy and contented, as he lay listening to the blasts of the storm outside and was glad he was sheltered there warm and snug and safe.

And then the stirring in the sick room, and the light which streamed from the half opened door, brought a sudden realization that Josie was still sick and they were far from help.

Panic seized hold of him. Would Josie die? Couldn't something be done to help her? If only her father were there, the good, kind Dr. Baker, who had a way of making everything all right. And yet the Great Physician Jesus was there. "O Jesus," he prayed, "please take care of her!"

And then silently getting to his feet he tiptoed to the door. He saw Aunt Ruth's tired and fearful face and Josie's flushed cheeks and heard her rapid breathing and her wild talk about sheep and something about the storm.

As he stood there, silent and unseen, Art decided what to do. Moving cautiously back to where he had been sleeping, he found his jacket and put it on. Pulling on his shoes and finding his flashlight he stepped to the door. There he stopped and bowed his head and prayed. Then, quietly opening the door, he stepped out onto the porch. The suddenness of the cold wind almost pushed him back, and holding onto the door he closed it even as he heard Aunt Ruth call. He ran across the porch and jumped down to the ground.

It was very dark and terribly cold. He stopped for a moment and hid behind the tree, as the cabin door opened behind him. He could see Aunt Ruth standing there, surrounded by light and staring into the dark storm and calling him to come back. The wind beat back her voice so that he could scarcely hear. With a sob she closed the door, and going to Josie's bed she fell to her knees and prayed for a child lost in the night, alone and afraid.

Art knew only that he must keep going, for if he stopped he would die. The cold wind blasted through his thick jacket with icy knife-like thrusts. He dropped to his knees and crawled over the flat rocks at the top of the mountain. The wind blew so hard there that he was almost knocked to the ground when he tried to stand up, and the ice was slippery. Moving cautiously forward, he slid unexpectedly down the other side of the slope and skidded to a stop against a huge fir tree at the edge of the forest. Stunned for a moment, he lay there and then with his face bitten by the sting of the snow, he got slowly to his feet and staggered toward the trees.

There the wind was not so strong, but the snow was blowing up drifts against the logs, drifts that came to his hips.

More than once, he stumbled and lay with the snow piled high on top of him. It was warm under the snow out of the wind and the cold, so warm, it seemed that he could lie there and sleep—sleep forever. Rousing himself, he struggled up and pushed on, down, down, down the mountain. A tree crashed suddenly ahead of him and he made his way slowly around it. Another tree, a great oak, cracked and roared to the ground with a resounding crash that shook the earth underneath him. This time he went straight on through the crunching branches, crawling up over the giant trunk and resting for a moment against it, out of the reach of the wind. Then on, on and on.

Art was cold, so cold that he couldn't seem to feel the cold any more. His back was numb so that he could scarcely feel his jacket; so cold that he didn't care. Josie was sick, yes, and he was trying to help her, but he couldn't. It was too big a job and he was too tired and too sleepy. Josie would be all right. He was all right. He would lie down now and sleep. Yes, sleep, sleep.

He was sinking down into the snow when he heard a voice. "Art," it said, "get up, quick, quick." He was so surprised that he forgot his weariness and jumped up and ran forward to see who had come to rescue him. But no one was there.

The wind was not quite so strong now, except when he crossed the meadows; and the brush was not quite so thick. And when he had almost given up hope of ever getting to the bottom of the mountain, he stumbled across a ditch and onto a road. He was down at last.

Just which way to go on the road he couldn't tell, but whichever way he went there would be a house. But it was midnight, and would the house be lighted? He turned to the left and stumbled along with the wind piercing and pushing him through the blackness.

Sure enough, there was a light, small and away from the road. He found the side road leading to it. He tried to run, but he was too tired. Moving forward slowly, too tired to think, he stumbled on until he stood on the porch and knocked. He tried to open it, but it was locked. Shouting and crying, he knocked and kicked at the door, but there was only silence inside. Sinking down onto the porch he sat there, too cold and tired to try more.

Mr. and Mrs. Gordon and Dr. and Mrs. Baker were sleeping well that night. It had been cold outside when they went to bed, but the weather reports had not said that it would rain or snow. Mr. Gordon woke up about one o'clock and was lying awake, faintly disturbed, but he didn't know why. Then suddenly he realized that it was snowing and a storm was raging outside. He was trying to decide whether to call the doctor and talk to him about whether the children would be all right in the snow. "But of course they are all right," he thought. "They have a cabin up there and blankets." But he couldn't seem to get back to sleep. Once he thought he heard a shout at the door, but finally decided that it was the wind. He noticed the reflection of light on the ceiling in his room and realized that he had forgotten to turn off the porch light.

Putting on his robe, he went downstairs and snapped off the light. Once again he thought he heard a faint noise on the porch. He opened the door, but nothing was there. He was about to close it when he saw something on the steps. Going closer he saw that it was a boy. He gave a shout of surprise and rushed out to pick him up. The boy was half frozen, or dead, he couldn't tell which. Carrying him into the light, he looked down into the blue face of Art Smith.

Shouting for the doctor, he began to rub Art's arms and legs and in a few moments Dr. Baker was there to help. It was perhaps five minutes later that Art opened his eyes and saw faces of his friends who loved him.

There was something he had come to tell them, but somehow he couldn't seem to remember what. He wanted to sleep now. He would remember later, perhaps. Something about Josie, he thought. Josie, yes, that was it. Something had happened to Josie. Josie was sick. Yes, that is why he had come. The words came slowly to his thick blue lips. "Josie's sick," he said and then darkness settled over him again.

The Rescue

THE STORM HAD ENDED and the sun was rising over the distant mountains when Dr. Baker and Mr. Gordon reached the little cabin at the top of the mountain.

Stamping across the porch they knocked at the door and called out, but there was no answer. The two men looked at each other with frightened glances.

"That's funny," Mr. Gordon said, and opened the door. The two men stepped inside.

There, huddled in a corner by the stove, were Betty and Bill asleep. "Shhh," whispered Mr. Gordon, "don't waken them."

Then, leading the way, he pushed open the door of the bedroom. Dr. Baker followed him, not knowing what they would find. Mr. Gordon stopped in the doorway and motioned for Dr. Baker to be quiet. Coming quietly into the room, the men saw Josie lying there with eyes closed, and at the side of the bed a lady was kneeling, crying. It was Aunt Ruth.

"We're here, Miss Ruth," Mr. Gordon said gently. She gave a little cry of welcome and then burst again into tears.

"I'm afraid it's too late," she sobbed. "Oh, I'm afraid it's too late!"

Dr. Baker was beside Josie now, listening to her chest. "No," he said grimly, "it's not too late. Please, God, please, don't let it be too late."

Quickly opening his black bag, he took out a bottle and a needle. And in a few moments he had thrust the needle deep into Josie's arm and forced into it the liquid that could save her life.

And then, with little else to do but wait and pray, Josie's daddy sat down beside her and he, too, wept, covering his face with his hands. Bill and Betty were awake now and came quietly into the room.

"Daddy!" Bill cried out. "When did you come?" And then he saw Josie's face white against the pillow.

"Oh, Daddy," he said fearfully, "I've been asleep! Josie's still sick. Oh, Daddy, will she be all right?"

"I don't know, Bill," Daddy said. "I think it's time to pray again." Then everyone got down on his knees and Mr. Gordon prayed. "O God, our Father," he said with deep earnestness, "help us now. Josie is very, very sick, but You can make her well if You want to. Please do—but Lord, we want Your will to be done. Help us to pray the way we should. We love Josie and we want her well and strong again. Please help her. In Jesus' name we ask this. Amen."

Then each of the others prayed, and last of all Josie's daddy.

The morning wore away. Sometimes it seemed to Dr. Baker that he couldn't stand it, sitting there listening to each breath. Yet the long morning did move slowly on, and by noon the doctor began to be hopeful. His face glowed with happy relief. "She's going to make it," he kept saying again and again, almost to himself. "She's going to be all right. Oh, thank You, Father!"

Toward midafternoon Josie opened her eyes and stared around her. She didn't seem to recognize Aunt Ruth, but as soon as she caught sight of Dr. Baker, her eyes sparkled.

"Oh, Daddy," she said, "you're here! I've been sick."

"Yes, little girl," her daddy said gently, "but you're better now. The Lord has given you back to us." And by suppertime that night Josie was wide-awake and chattering happily. And so it was a happy evening instead of the sad one that Aunt Ruth had feared.

Josie was getting well so fast that Dr. Baker decided he could go back home, since there wasn't any extra place to sleep in the cabin. He and Mr. Gordon said good night, and taking their lanterns, went down the trail on the other side of the mountain, leaving the children and Aunt Ruth until morning. And soon everyone in the cabin grew sleepy and decided it was time for bed, and before you could blink twice they were fast asleep.

Josie was the first to awaken the next morning. She felt fine. She wanted to jump up and waken everyone else, but Daddy had told her to stay in bed, so she did. She lay there quietly, thinking about how ill she had been and about Art. How anxious she was to see him, and to tell him that she was sorry for all the bad things she had thought about him! "He'll be glad, too," she thought. And then she prayed again for him. Art had done a brave and wonderful thing in going down in the storm, and she was glad that he was her friend.

After what seemed like a long, long time to Josie, the others woke up and Aunt Ruth began making pancakes for breakfast. Bill said that they were the very best pancakes he had eaten in all his whole life. He had just finished eating his tenth one, and was beginning to feel full, when they heard Dr. Baker and Mr. Gordon and some other men outside. Dashing to the door, they saw that the two men had brought a stretcher to carry Josie down the trail.

Quickly finishing breakfast and washing up the dishes, they were ready to go. Mr. Gordon had brought along a heavy sweater for Bill and a fur coat of Mrs. Gordon's for Aunt Ruth to wear. They covered up Josie with blankets and Josie was snug and warm.

Then the little party locked the cabin door and started slowly down the trail.

It was slow work keeping Josie from sliding off the stretcher, because the trail was rough and steep. Josie didn't mind at all. She thought it was a wonderful way to go down a mountain! But her daddy and Mr. Gordon weren't quite so sure!

Finally they came to the bottom of the mountain where Dr. Baker's car was parked, and piling in, they were soon driving up the Gordons' road happily singing as they went.

Josie became quiet as they climbed out of the car at the Gordons' farm. She was partly glad and partly sorry when only Mrs. Gordon came rushing out to welcome her back. Art was at a neighbor's because Mrs. Gordon had asked him to run an errand for her. Josie didn't know how Art would feel toward someone who had hated him and said such mean things about him. She didn't have long to wait. The door suddenly opened and in bounced Art. He took one look around the room and saw Josie standing there, looking a little frightened and embarrassed.

"Yippee," yelled Art, and ran over to Josie and began to dance circles around her in his excitement and joy in seeing Josie back.

Everyone laughed and soon the room was full of laughter and happiness. It was Bill who suggested that they all have prayer together.

And as each one prayed, it seemed to them all that the very glory of Heaven was there in the room. And it was, for the Lord Jesus was there—the same Lord Jesus who had heard Bill's prayer and had become Art's Friend and Josie's too—a Friend and a Shepherd.